## *REVIEWS OF*

Many of us have borne witness to buffalo being shot while searching for food outside Yellowstone's borders in the depths of hard winters. All of us know the connection between the buffalo and the Tribes. But how many of us are aware of the effect of the slaughter on the Tribes' wish for the Park's excess buffalo alive, or the necessity of the meat of the slaughtered to feed the hungry on the Reservations?

Shari Nault's characters come together when the Blackfeet are called to butcher the slain animals. Running the gamut from holy man to renegade, all of them find themselves outlaws against unjust law. White man's law.

In a suspenseful story of hiding out in the Park in the dead of winter, of plotting a takeover of the park—a take-back of the park, of trying to honor the animal who is kin, of warriors who cannot stay out of trouble no matter what they do, of the never-ending white suspicion of the Indian, of the annoying tough white woman who comes to the rescue, of the nobility of the Tribes' leaders, Nault hasn't left out much. Palpably capturing what winter in Yellowstone feels like, she also exposes the tenuousness of the Indian/White understanding, while forcefully presenting the power of Indian ritual in the face of American bureaucracy.

*Ruth Rudner has written about the American West for many years for the Wall Street Journal's "Leisure & Arts" page. In her book of essays, A Chorus of Buffalo, she explores the theme of the buffalo and its world. Her other books include Ask Now The Beasts; Partings; Greetings From Wisdom, Montana.*

I read Shari Nault's 'Buffalo Tango' while staying with friends in Red Lodge, Montana. I was captivated by its well-drawn characters to such an extent that I wanted to be Feral and was totally smitten by the gorgeous Gabe. The dialogue is sparkling and witty and

I found myself laughing out loud on more than one occasion.

But the book also deals with the very serious subjects of buffalo conservation and the treatment of North American Indians.

I am from England; a climber and world traveller and consider myself to be a well-educated woman but Shari's book made me realise how little I knew about the harsh realities faced by both buffalo and Indian. All in all, I found it to be a humorous, tender and informative read.

*Jules McGowan, Nettleton, North Lincolnshire, United Kingdom*

As a former wildlife biologist,with a long history of working with Native people in my business, Buffalo Tango was spot on the issues. But what I most enjoyed were the characters. I thought about them even when I wasn't reading the book. They were so real. I want to know what happens next. Hurry up and finish the next book Shari.

*David Gylten, Mountain Ridge Trading*

# Buffalo Tango

Mike & Margie

Enjoy!

Shari

shari nault

Published by French Coyote Press

This is a work of fiction. Names, characters, places and incidents either are products of the author's imagination or are used fictitiously. Any resemblance to actual events or locales or persons, living or dead, is entirely coincidental.

This book is published by French Coyote Press.


Manufactured in the United States of America.
ISBN- 0-9966713-0-7
ISBN- 9 78-0-9966713-0-9

# DEDICATION

I dedicate this work to my three daughters; Holly who shows me determination, Heidi who never sees an obstacle and Kim whose faith in the Almighty and me never falters. To my husband David whose kindness gives me shelter. There are my friends on the "Rez," who probably wish to remain nameless. And always, my father Andy whose boldness and craziness gave me insight into my characters.

## NOTE FROM THE AUTHOR

This is purely a work of fiction but the circumstances are true. Since 1985, over 8,500 buffalo have been shot as they left Yellowstone National Park in search of food. In the winter of 2007/08, more than 1,600 were killed. The research states that there has not been one case of Brucellosis transmitted from buffalo to cattle, while elk carrying the disease are not restrained, hazed or shot. What is at the heart of this – is it actually a cattle health issue or a grazing rights issue. There has been progress made with more Indian tribes receiving buffalo, but it has been, and is, a struggle. The other question the book explores is what it means to be a Native American in the 21st Century.

## HISTORIC POLICY SHIFT

"Wild bison will be allowed to migrate out of Yellowstone National Park and stay in parts of Montana year-round under a December 22, 2015, move by Gov. Steve Bullock that breaks a longstanding impasse in a wildlife conflict that's dragged on for decades. The Democratic governor's decision likely won't end the periodic slaughters of some bison that roam outside Yellowstone in search of food at lower elevations. But it for the first time allows hundreds of the animals to linger year-round on an estimated 400 square miles north and west of the park."

*The Billings Gazette*, *Billings Montana*

# CHAPTER 1

## THE SACRED

January 5, 2009
Outside the borders of Yellowstone National Park
Minus (-23) twenty-three degrees

Leroy, his cheeks bluish-red from the cold, sucked his lips in around the gaps in his teeth. Slowly he stomped a crusty snow path in front of the tipi for Old Man and the others. The brown flaps of his hat, untied over his protruding ears, gave him the look of a hound dog about to take flight. Feeling the cold numb his nose while rivets of misery soaked his jacket, he wished he could slip back to the pickup and sleep. Better yet, go back home to Darlene's breasts pressed hot against his chest giving him a sweet reason to sweat. Last night's whiskey comfort had worn thin.

They had driven half the night, put the tipi up by the light of a flashlight and crawled dumb-tired into their sleeping bags. “What in the hell is so sacred about butchering buffalo at dawn,” he muttered. But he knew Old Man would consider nothing else. The Park Service liked it because the television crews and the animal rights people were still snug under a blanket or nursing their coffee at the café this time of morning.

He wished he had learned some nice indoor work in prison like plumbing or barbering instead of butchering. Scanning the tree line edging the circle of dark mound carcasses, he saw a coyote shimmering in the first light. Tail down, he was slinking in and out of the brush like an uninvited relative. “Wait your turn little brother, we will all eat.”

Kneeling by the fire, feeling the heat singe his face, Paul Heavy Shield spooned grounds into the blackened enamel pot and breathed in the rich smell of boiling coffee. It felt good to be on the land even in this cold. When he was a kid his grandfather, Thomas Heavy Shield, would take him hunting in the back country. There was plenty of game to shoot in those days. They would put up a small tent and stay out for a week or more. Grandfather ran a trap line; two dollars for a coyote, five for a cross-fox. Paul snared rabbits. The first time he heard a caught rabbit scream, it sounded like a woman being tortured. He wanted to quit. But his grandfather spoke to him of hunter and prey and the respect due each.

On one trip Paul insisted on bringing his dog Skunk. The Old One was not happy, “Dogs raised on table scraps cannot protect themselves against animals who live by their wits," Heavy Shield cautioned. Skunk had a way of getting himself between a rock and big trouble. Paul hid his pet under the sleeping bags until they were out of town.

Late that night Skunk barked furiously to get out. Before Thomas could stop him, Paul opened the tent flap and in an instant the wolverine had the dog's nose clamped in his fierce jaws. Skunk lurched backwards dragging the wolverine into the tent. Leaping to their feet, Grandfather and Paul were knocked back by the flying Skunk as the fury with the two white stripes down his back flung the terrified dog back and forth shaking him like a bag of dirt. Dark as a cave, the small tent bulged with howls of pain and the wolverine's hiss along with the clatter of cooking utensils, traps and gear coming in contact with Skunk and the whirling wolverine. The beast tore at the dog's belly and shredded the sleeping bags with his sharp claws. The terrible stink of the crazed animals fogged the air bad enough to drive a vulture off roadkill. Finding the flashlight while scrambling for his rifle, Paul saw his grandfather raise a hatchet high over his head. With a wild whoop he came down square on the skull of the wolverine. It still took a crowbar to free the dog from the terrible jaws.

"The wolverine is smaller than your dog, but he will attack the bear and the bear will run," Grandfather said. "They kill and don't eat. Wolverine tear up and soil a trap line and bait and never get caught. Their spirits are like that of a bad, mean man. You are lucky he didn't grab your nose." Paul paid heed to his grandfather's predictions after that.

Sipping coffee this morning, he wondered if Grandfather had summoned the wicked wolverine, the wild terror, to teach him a lesson.

Paul had come back home less than a year ago. Back to the rez to live his beliefs. Six years he'd been away at college, another ten as a schoolteacher in Seattle. When he first went to the city, he had belonged to Indian political groups determined to challenge the system. By the time he left, he had even quit playing basketball at the red ghetto gym, the only place left to do battle, to count coup. The wolverine haunted his dreams; shredded his life. He had to go back. But once home, he felt like a hundred buffalo robes were piled on him, shielding,

comforting, but suffocating. Alcoholism, no work, physical and social abuse on the rez was sucking the life out of many of his tribe. Even chronic pain can be a comfort for its familiarity. The reservations were both a strong community and a trap. His job at Head Start was to open their minds to options while respecting what was.

Today, for a change, he felt good about the work to be done. His people needed the meat. This time they would not come home empty-handed. This was his third trip to Yellowstone, to a kill site. The Park Service sighting buffalo outside the protective boundaries of the Park would notify each tribe in turn, giving them twelve hours to gather a butchering crew and get here. If the buffalo went back into the Park before they arrived, they would wait. After three days in a motel, all their cash gone, the gatherers would usually go home driving the long miles in silence. No eyes met to mirror their disappointment. Each mile bringing them closer to the hungry, hopeless looks. White guys were always talking about "those Indians gettin' all the government money, livin high." He wished he could meet some of those rich Indians, he'd ask 'em for a loan.

While not a hunter, as director of the Head Start program, Paul felt it was up to him to provide food so kids could learn. The shelves were often bare. The Government, by subsidizing the dairy industry, did give the school butter, milk and something that looked like big logs of cheese. At least he thought it was cheese. Hard to know. That and bread, lots and lots of white bread and rice and beans. Too many starchy staples at his table he thought as he sat back on his heels, cursing the paunch folding over his belt. He had gained 30 pounds since he had come back. Government rations, commodities, fill the belly, but don't satisfy hunger. I have to do better by the young. They will grow up thinking all nourishment comes from "commods," not given freely by the earth.

Gazing across the meadow to where the Park Service had shot a line of buffalo as they crossed the border leaving Yellowstone, he wished the kill site was like the old hunt days. His grandfather told of riding into a herd on his swiftest pony to bring down the fattest. Now there is no integrity between hunter and prey – no respect for the balance demonstrated by Mother Earth to all her creatures. Now federal game wardens hazed then killed buffalo as they followed the snowmobile trails out of Yellowstone Park in search of food. The animals were starving in the Park, but because ranchers were scared the buffalo carried disease to their cattle, the Feds wholesale slaughtered them. The count was up to 800 animals this winter alone and there were still cold months ahead. Rather than let the meat go to waste, the tribes, unafraid of Brucellosis, salvaged the carcasses. At least this way the buffalo could feed the People, the role given them by the creator.

Like the campfire that burned Paul's front while the wind and cold scraped his backside, his people would eat, but his culture would not be nourished. Before they touched the carcasses the Old Man would ask the buffalos' forgiveness and honor them with ceremony in hope of retribution. It was their way.

Gabe soon joined Leroy trampling the snow flat in front of the tipi, a primitive dance in the white shrouded meadow. Paul snickered as Gabe took the lead and Leroy slowed to a shuffle. His cheeks folded into jowls that swayed with each bob of his head. Just like an old Bloodhound, thought Paul. Better watch out for the wolverine.

Later, squatting around the campfire, the men warmed their hands around hot coffee mugs. Gabe Dumont's black eyes reflected the flames, anger masked his carved features. His long black hair was knotted in a single braid, a grizzly claw encased in silver hung around his neck. Tall, sinewy muscled, he took his striking looks for granted. Performing occasionally as a movie stunt rider he picked up extra money and was offered plenty of free love. But wildlife and wildland, not wild women, had his interest.

"Where do the Feds get off trying to manage buffalo anyway?" Gabe said. His voice had the weariness of repetition. "I've got the same education as those agents and a lot more work in the field. I spent half my time here as a kid. This is my place. Those bastards just won't listen. Instead of killing buffalo, give them to the tribes to build their herds. We could feed our people if the politicians would listen.

"It's a mess," he continued, "they should relocate about half of the Yellowstone game just to feed what is left. Way too many elk. Moose eating the bark off trees. Bears and wolves are the only ones thriving, living off winter kill."

"Kinda reminds me of the reservation," sneered Paul. "Starve em slowly until we are too weak to resist. We will all die out in the name of system management." His voice trailed off as the flap on the tipi slowly opened and Old Man emerged, his back bent as a snow burdened willow, his lips moving in silent prayer. Grey braids wrapped in rich brown otter fur contrasted with the red and blue-striped capote covering him well past his knees. On his feet were tall leather beaded moccasins. He stood for a moment greeting the first light. The men snuffed out their cigarettes and waited expectantly.

Old Man unfolded a buffalo robe on the packed snow before the tipi. Reaching inside he withdrew three bundles wrapped in buckskin tied with leather thongs. Untying the sinew he carefully laid out a smudge stick of sage and pine needles, a braid of sweet grass, an eagle feather, buffalo horn and a sacred bone whistle. Unwrapping the next, Old Man grinned and pointing to two small stones on either side of a larger flint rock all in the shape of a buffalo, he said, "Young ones, good, there are new, young ones the rocks make more." The last bundle lay before him in front of the fire. Once more he leaned into the tipi bringing out a small drum which he handed to Paul.

Forming a cross-legged circle, the men begin to chant low to the drum's rhythmic lead. Purifying himself by waving the smoke from the smudge over his face and chest, Old Man invited each to do so. Then, unwrapping the final bundle,

Old Man lit and then offered the pipe to the four directions. The smoke curled around the bowl lifting their prayers to the heavens. Passing the pipe east to Gabe he said in Pikani-Blackfeet, "It is good that we are welcomed by the sun, the sun sent Napi to give us the medicine pipe long ago."

A breeze whipped the snow into sharp edges stinging their faces. Paul's brown fingers lightly caressed the drum, now faster, stronger, weaving a cadence, a rhythmic trail, to follow. His braids brushed across the taunt leather with a whisper.

Gabe drew deeply on the pipe, smoke softening around his full lips. He passed it to Leroy. Then Paul passed the pipe back to Old Man. In the meadow behind them the wind stirred the quaking aspens creating the sound of a thousand rattles matching the drum reverberating against the stillness of the meadow. 

Wood smoke and smoldering sweet grass mingling with the grog of coffee bit their frosty nostrils. Raising his hands, palms toward them, the Old Man spoke in Pikuni - Blackfeet. "Go. It is time. The buffalo's spirits are now free to roam and they offer their bodies that we might live. Go, do your work with honor." Lowering his head, he resumed chanting, his hands shaping the meaning, echoing across the valley.

Trudging back to where the pickups were parked, Paul and Gabe grabbed a tarp out of the back of the rig and tossed on saws, axes, boxes and gunny sacks. Folding it travois style, they drug it through the heavy drifts, quiet, heads down, past the tipi and the praying elder. Soon the heavy thud of an ax striking bone echoed across the white expanse. Reluctant to leave the warm fire, Leroy poured another cup of coffee scalding his throat as he gulped it down. Coughing he slogged toward the others.

"I'm telling you prison screwed me over in more ways," Leroy grunted as he skinned the heavy hide away from the flesh. "I kept telling 'em, I'm Injun, don't give me no knives, unless you want me to use 'em on your scalp. I want to learn something like wash machine repair. Maybe be like the lonely Maytag guy on TV. All warm working inside, bored, but warm. Not this shit."

"The way I see it, Gabe said, "the Park Service just wants to sit around and count elk turds. They ought to open to limited hunting. With this overgrazing why the hell not have a hunting season for tribes only. Although my stomach don't much care what season it is." He cut the flesh away carefully. A nick in the hide would lower the quality of the robe. The carcass was beginning to freeze and he was losing feeling in his hands. Feeling a slight prick, he held his arm up in the light. "Checking to see if I've still got all my fingers," he snickered.

"Why can't we load them on the truck and butcher back at our own rez," said Leroy brightening."

" Leroy, you are a dumb ass," taunted Gabe. "How they gonna fit? Run alongside? How are we gonna lift 1,500 pounds of deadweight? The heads alone weigh 300 pounds. One of these wet hides skinned out, 200 pounds easy. Got anymore big ideas?"

"We do need some new hunting grounds," said Paul ignoring Leroy and tossing Gabe a gunny sack to wipe his hands. "Nothing left to shoot on the rez."

"Two down, five to go," muttered Leroy. "How come the wardens always pick a spot where the snow is five feet deep and a mile from the road to do the kill," he whined as he sat down on a carcass and lit a cigarette. Suddenly behind him, they heard a rustle, a snort and the tear of material. Leroy yelped as a sharp pain raked his back.

"Get away," yelled Gabe as he grabbed his rifle and fired at a buffalo struggling to stand in the deep snow directly behind Leroy. Bellowing his rage, the beast swung his great head knocking Leroy to the ground. Leroy laid there waiting for the final crush of the huge head. Squinting through closed eyes he saw Gabe swing on to the back of the swaying animal. As the buffalo threw his head back to dislodge his passenger, Gabe hugged his neck with one arm and cut his throat with the other. Crumbling to its knees, the old bull sighed and rolled over. A stream of red pumped into the white snow. Gabe wrenched his arm from under its neck, climbed off nonchalantly, tipped his hat and yelled, "The champion bull rider is Gabe Dumont! Now get up off your ass Leroy and get to work."

As the pale sun moved sluggish across the horizon, its rays promising but never warming, the songs of the elder blended into the silent corners filling the expanse. Working stiff and quiet against the cold the men wrestled the bloody meat quarters onto the tarp. Smaller pieces they threw in boxes or gunny sacks. Hides were stacked to the side.

Gradually a buzzing, incessant whine of engine noise stung the air. Looking up from their work toward the mouth of the narrow meadow they could make out a small buffalo herd struggling to stay ahead of two snow machines pushing them into a stampede. In the rear, a calf, separated from its mother and bawling its distress, was floundering, finally slipping from view in the churning drifts. As the lunging animals grew closer and glimpsed the butchering camp they turned sharply stumbling against each other, wallowing in the deep snow. Their terrified wails a crescendo against of the high pitch of the machines.

The elder's shrill voice pierced the bedlam – a garble between English and Indian. Waving his arms wildly, he began to run toward the herd closing the distance between the tipi and the center of the meadow.

Dropping their tools, Paul, Gabe and Leroy stared in angry frustration as the snow machines hurled by circling the animal's flank. Suddenly the herd broke rank heading toward the clearing where the trucks were parked. The rustlers gunned it. With pistons screaming they swung around and throttled full out to cut off the panicked animals and push them back to the deep snow.

Blindly the herd swung towards Old Man. Facing the wild-eyed massive beasts bearing down on him, the elder folded his arms across his chest and stood fast. Transfixed, the three Indians covered in butchering blood stared as the snow churning white shrouded buffalo seemingly suspended between earth and sky - closed the distance toward their holy one.

Gabe staggered against the deafening crescendo of the buffalos' terror as they struggled through the snow toward Old Man. Roaring engines and his own rage pushed him through the drifts. Paul and Leroy, stunned into silence, felt the world hold its breath. The lead bull, breaking snow with his massive shoulders, stopped square in front of Old Man, their heads seeming to touch, Wise one to Wise one, eye-to-eye. Old Man stood fast. Old Bull stood guard. The herd parted a channel around them.

"Let's go run those assholes outa here," yelled Gabe after the snowmobilers as he sloughed through the heavy snow toward their truck. Paul, reaching Old Man, saw him talking softly to the huge beast. In a moment, the bull turned and brushing shoulders with Old Man, followed the herd.

Paul broke a trail for Old Man to return to the tipi while Gabe and Leroy started the pickup. Sluggish in the deepening cold, the engine sputtered and finally caught just as Paul slid in. Gabe floored the throttle, sliding sideways until the tires caught on the gravel edging the road. Cranking the wheel with the tires spitting out snow and rocks he goosed the pickup onto the plowed hard-pack. Punching the gas pedal he cursed as the back end swung around trying to swap leads. Alternately skidding, then grabbing where there was gravel, they raced down the road finally running parallel with the herd while the snow machines flanked the other side. "Lets get 'em," gritted Gabe.

"Slow down," yelled Leroy as they approached a road sign warning a blind curve. Paul gripped the dashboard. Sliding the width of the turn, Gabe eased off the gas and pulled the nose right murmuring, "Whoa pony, steady." Leroy slumped in his seat and pulled his cap lower. "Ridin' with you is like ridin a green bronc," he muttered.

Rounding the bend, the truck skidded, left the road and climbed more than half way up the embankment. They were stuck. "Stay here," Gabe said. Climbing into the truck bed, he grabbed a rope and threw a lasso around the closest snow machine's rear seat and gave a yank. Pulling the rope tight around the pickup's ball hitch, it held while the machine kept going. Just for a couple of seconds. Then the front end jerked up like a calf hitting the end of the branding rope and the rider on the front seat hit the packed snow hard. The other snow machine was coming up fast – fast enough to run over the rider on the ground without even seeing him. A yell and it was all over. Gabe dropped the rope. The second machine continued toward the runaway sled.

A moment later there was a huge jolt and Paul and Leroy instinctively covered their faces as the windshield shattered. Straddling the truck like a giant hood ornament, the dazed buffalo shifted his bulk rocking the pickup as he strained to free himself. Glazed black eyes stared at them through the fractured glass. The massive shaggy head was magnified by a thousand prisms. "Get out before we are crushed," yelled Leroy.

"No, stay put, this rig is tough," yelled Paul as he tentatively rolled down the window and leaned through the opening. Looking toward the meadow he dropped quickly back inside and said, "We got trouble now." Across the field, the driver-less snow machine was trying to climb a tree, all roar and no traction. The driver on the ground was yelling, holding his leg, blood soaking a circle around him.

Leroy reached in a bag lying on the floor at Paul's feet saying, "Time for a little blue thunder, gonna blow them a new one."

As the other driver turned his sled and headed toward him, Gabe glanced back. Paul and Leroy were struggling with the jammed door. Cussing, Paul threw his shoulder against it half falling out as the door finally gave. The buffalo, rocking back and forth on the hood, finally freed himself and with a shrug waddled down the road trailing the herd that was quickly disappearing.

"What are ya doin here, do you injuns own these buffalo," snarled the snowmobiler slowly crawling off his machine. Goggles hid his face, his hat was pulled low and a scarf covered his neck and chin. Reaching behind the seat he grabbed a rifle and loaded a shell in the chamber.

"They belong to no one," stated Gabriel, his voice low. Paul moved closer and Leroy raised his rifle.

"Then what is your problem," said the snowmobiler, "you miserable Indians think you still own this country and all that's in it and I say get your sorry red asses back in the truck and get out of my way. I've got me some buffalo to chase and they are getting away." His voice trailed off as he stared in disbelief at his partner lying on the ground. "What the hell! Did you shoot my buddy?" the snowmobiler yelled.

"You ran over him."

"Jerry, I'm hurt bad," he moaned.

"Like hell I did! You prairie niggers trying to kill us! Back away," he snarled waving the rifle at them.

Dropping to his knees, he grabbed his partner by the shoulders and tried to make him sit up but the injured man pushed him away moaning, "My leg, my leg."

Whirling around, the snowmobiler turned the rifle on them

and yelled, "You pick him up and tie him on my sled or die."

Laying the rifle on the fender, Leroy, Paul and Gabe approached the injured man. "Put that rifle down and help," said Paul.

"No way. Get my buddy on that sled. I'm not letting go of this gun," said the snowmobiler. His wild eyes jerked between the men and his friend.

"He's not going to stay on," said Gabe as he stepped back. "We need to tie him to you."

A bullet hit a tree branch above Gabe's head dumping a load of snow. The snowmobiler pulled the rifle level with Gabe's chest, "Don't mess with me that was a warning - the last one."

"Help me," the injured man pleaded.

Propping the rifle against his machine, the snowmobiler reached for his buddy. Leroy, grabbing his own rifle off the fender yelled, "Okay, who is calling the shots now?"

"I knew it, you're gonna kill us both. Well, I'm getting the hell out here," said the snowmobiler while he backed away and jumped on his machine. "I'll bring help, you hear me Skip," he yelled over his shoulder as he swerved around the pickup. "I'll get you," snarled the driver as he punched the throttle and the machine sped away down the icy road. The three men watched it fade from view.

"Leroy, you dumb shit, put the rifle down," commanded Gabriel. Leroy meekly put the firearm back and mumbling took his place beside Paul.

"Got to get him to the hospital," said Paul as he and Gabe lay the victim in the back of the pickup. Covering him with a sleeping bag and an old tarp, Paul said, "Let's get him to my truck quick."

Gabe backed the pickup off the embankment while Paul and Leroy pushed. Surveying the truck's undercarriage, he said, "We better travel with a case of oil, cause the pan is bent and it is sure to leak, but the axle seems okay. We'll pick up Old Man and come back in the morning for the meat. Got a bad feeling about this mess. Bet he goes to the cops."

"We didn't do nothin," whined Leroy. "They caused all the trouble. But I'm gonna grab that lasso off that tree-climin sled just cause I am."

"We will know soon enough," said Paul.

"Should have shot both them sled heads and buried them with their miserable machines," snarled Gabe as he eased the truck around and started back toward camp.

# CHAPTER 2

# YOU AIN'T NO FRIEND OF MINE

"You ain't nothin' but a hound dog." At the refrain, Leroy, holding himself up with the jukebox, threw back his head and howled. Then, lurching forward, he fell into his beer foam. "Cryin' all the time." Pushing upright, he stumbled to a table where his friends Chester and Marie were nursing a long neck, passing it back and forth, taking measure of each pull on the bottle.

"Are you hearing me," he demanded leaning forward in the space between them, his boozy breath covering them with stink. "I'm telling you something important. They were trying to kill all them buffalo, run 'em until their lungs burst from the cold and fear. We didn't mean to hurt anybody. We was just protecting our brothers. But nobody ever believes me," he lamented. "I figure them cops will show up pretty quick," he said and slumped in the chair beside Marie.

"Maybe this time I'll train to be the Maytag guy."

"What's a Maytag guy?" murmured Marie.

Leroy's response was buried in the "Ohhh, eeh," howl of the hound dog verse, "You ain't never caught a rabbit and you ain't no friend of mine." His voice trailed off as the first lawman filled the frame of the saloon door. Taking a step into the room, the officer's beefy swagger brought a pall of silence to the party.

Watching the cop quiz the bartender while the second lawman surveyed the room, Leroy staggered back to the jukebox swaying to the music. Keeping a watch through slit eyes he hummed, "And you ain't no friend of mine." With a final "ohh-eeh" while raising his beer to his virtuoso accomplishment, Leroy slid to the floor, a pile of buffalo blood stained clothes cloaked in inevitable surrender. The bar emptied out the back door.

"Are you Leroy LaRue?" the burly officer asked, nudging Leroy with the pointed toe of his cowboy boot.

"What's it to ya," slurred Leroy. "I ain't nothin' but a hound dog," he hummed low.

"What's all the blood?" Kill somebody," the officer asked quietly.

"It ain't our fault. We never run over him."

Leroy struggled to sit up, indignation fueling his backbone. "They was chasing our buffalo on them dirty machines, but we never hurt nobody," he yelled. "In fact, we took him to the hospital when his buddy high-tailed it down the h-i-g-h-way," he stretched out the word like a short rope and hung on it.

"Were you in Yellowstone today?" the officer continued, his drilling boring a hole through Leroy's stupor.

"I sure was. About froze my ass off butchering those poor buffalo you Feds killed to take to my starving family."

"Did you pull a gun on the injured man's companion?" the officer's tone sharpened.

"He did it first," quipped Leroy and then laid back down curling into a fetal position.

The officer squatted down next to Leroy pushing his shoulder back to bring his face into clear view. "Did you threaten him?"

Blinking hard from the harsh overhead lights, Leroy's foggy eyes cleared for an instant. "With his sorry life," he said.

Sheriff Sam Norman stood up and nodding to the rookie behind him, headed for the door, saying, "Cuff him and book him. Oh, and read him his rights."

##

Sitting in the truck outside the hospital Paul watched his breath make swirly ice patterns on the windshield. The afternoon was fading into twilight. Should he go back in or find a pay phone and just call. He wasn't sure how long they'd keep the guy here in West Yellowstone. If he was hurt real bad, they would probably take him to Billings. The small staff had been so preoccupied with the patient that Paul had slipped out before they had a chance to question him.

He wondered where Gabe was. "He's a hot head, hope Old Man talks him down," Paul said to himself. "Leroy would head for the nearest tavern." Paul had taken to talking to himself after he first left the rez. Living lonely in the city, he longed to hear the soft syllables of the Indian tongue, even if it was just his own. "Head downtown, get a bite and call and see if Gabe and Old Man got home." Taking a drag off his cigarette, Paul started the engine and slowly began backing out of the lot, the cold heater blasting frigid air. Suddenly the door on his side jerked open.

"Going someplace?" asked Sheriff Sam Norman as he reached inside and turned off the key killing the engine. "I think we've got some things to talk about and your buddy Leroy is mighty lonely for your company."

CHAPTER 3

# COYOTE, RAVEN & HAWK BATTLE

A tavern across the street from Montana State University Stadium.

"You rode hard, you rode real fast, but I guess you didn't ride real good," sneered Red the Blackfeet cowboy, his pock-pitted face reflecting a green sheen from the neon beer sign blinking overhead.

Billy, the Sioux, kept his head down and fingered the beads on his belt, tracing the silver buckle that spoke to another time when he had ridden the best.

Dark looks flashed between him and the Blackfeet bronc

rider. "Wow, don't scare ole Red like that, said the Blackfeet. "We all been kicking your ass since the old, old, days and we can do it again," he boasted. "But just maybe not tonight," he grinned.

The saloon was filled with cowboys swaggering with winnings or sniveling in their beer over entry fees lost and nothing to take home for brag. The winter championship rodeo finals finished tonight and there would be no chance to make good till summer.

As the last twang of Waylon's, "Mamas, Don't Let Your Babies Grow Up to be Cowboys," faded the singer stepped from the stage and began to make her way through the crowd to the bar for a drink. "My mouth's so dry, it feels like I been sucking on a sock," she muttered. Passing the table where the Indian rodeo riders had congregated, she spied the top dollar winner from the Crow reservation. "Bet you'd be good for a stiff one," she said leaning over his shoulder. Her heavy breasts strained against the thin fabric of her sequined halter top. Resting on his shoulders, both pendulums slid slowly down circling his neck, framing his face revealing the view of her imprinted nipples grazing the shiny snaps on his shirt pockets. Red lips brushed his ear, bottle blond hair swayed in front of his face. "Hey cowboy," she drawled warm breath on his ear, "you are one hell of a bronc rider. How about you buying me a drink to celebrate." Pete stared straight ahead, his face warming to the color of her painted lips.

"Yo, Pete, didn't quit buyin did you," challenged Red as

the waitress passed around the burgers, hesitated, then placed the check in the middle of the table. "You won our share tonight, so it seems only right that you buy. Consider us your guests this being Crow Country and all."

Kenny, hanging out at the bar, heard the words, "buyin'" and sat himself down at the end of the table. Wandering the streets, no food, no sleep, was wearing on him. He figured Indians need to stick together, take care of each other. Cheyenne always welcome.

"Good thing I know how to ride a bronc, uphold Indian honor," retorted Pete, his face flushed from beer, breasts and high stakes. He carefully checked his new white cowboy hat for lipstick marks. Dammit, there it was.

He tipped back his chair forcing the woman to step back. Her high heel caught in a crack in the floorboard causing her to lurch against the next table where two rawboned cowboys sat hunched silent over their drinks. Casting a sideways glance from under the brim of their hats, they picked up their glasses and left, muttering, "Damn drunk Indians."

Red laughed and reaching over, pulled the singer onto his lap. Tipping his beer to her mouth he said, "Hey, you looking for a warrior, sing for ole Red."

Shoving back away from the table and sloshing beer over the food, Billy stood up and stared across at the Crow. His shiny red jacket with the blue embroidered letters "Sioux Country" glistened. "You saying you got the only honor at this table?" Sweat lined his upper lip, his eyes bulged.

"How can the Crow speak to honor anyway," said Billy's younger brother Jake who stood up beside Billy.

"Oh, Billy, not the Custer gig, again. Haven't you Sioux done anything since," Pete snickered. Jake threw his cowboy hat down shouting "That's it, it's Crow stew time."

"This isn't about our grandfather's time. Where were you in the 70s," challenged Billy, "when we were in the bunkers at Wounded Knee getting our asses shot off by the FBI over Indian rights? I'll tell you where, you Crows were sucking up to the government and getting special privileges, that's where."

"Wouldn't have lost to Feds if there had been more Blackfeet," added Red.

"Billy, Jake, sit down," said Pete. "Have another beer, eat your burger. Maybe Red will be generous when we come to Blackfeet Country and leave with all winnings." Billy stood glaring for a minute, then seeing that Pete and Red had lost interest, he and Jake sat down and picked up their burgers.

The ten o'clock news blared from the television positioned over the bar. *"Confiscated buffalo carcasses are being held at the Gardiner ranger station meat lockers,"* read the newscaster. *"What the tribes were promised was food for hungry people on the reservations is now being held as evidence against two of their members. One of the instigators of the incident is still at large."*

"Caught one of the skins, a Sioux," added Red with a sideline glare toward Billy. "The one that got away is my woman's cousin. He is Tribal Fish & Game from my country.

"Hot damn," he hollered pounding the table and shoving the woman to her feet, "that meat was headed for Browning and we need it."

The singer staggered, knocking into the next table. Watching from the bar, the drummer slammed his beer down and headed toward them yelling "You can't push her around."

She blocked him shoving him back toward the stage muttering, "There are five of them, you fool." Red, intent on his mission, never even noticed the advance or the retreat.

"We could use some of that meat," said Billy, glaring at Red across the table.

"I say we go get it then," Red commanded looking around the circle. "Who is in?"

One by one they nodded. At the Crow's turn, he quickly injected, "How about another beer."

"Better get it to go, make it a six pack each and a carton of Camels, my generous host," laughed Red as he steered Pete toward the cash register.

Handing over three twenty dollar bills, Pete edged toward the door. "Go get my truck started, check on my horse," he said ducking out.

On his way out the door to the parking lot, Red stopped and plugged four quarters from the Crow's change into the poker machine. Lights blinked, fruit spun in dizzy colors. No dice. "All flash but no cash," he muttered, "just like the rodeo."

The parking lot was a haze of blue smoke as one by one the warriors fired up their trusty steeds. Mufflers growled a gravely chorus. In the din, Red cranked the starter and stomped on the gas pedal but the engine only coughed and spewed black carbon. The battery of his 04 Ford pickup weakened with each turn. "Piece of shit government issue."

"Hey brother," the Blackfeet called to the Sioux parked next to him, "can you spare ole Red a jump?"

Billy looked over at his ancient enemy, his lip curling in a sneer. "Guess we won't be picking on my Pinto anymore, huh. Oh, what the hell," he said finally reaching in the backseat for the jumper cables. Kenny was sacked out snoring.

Circling their cars, Red yelled over the engine's noise. "We stay together. It's about an hour from here. Take the Gardiner exit off I-90. We meet at the Blue Tongue Tavern. Figure our plan from there." The caravan roared out of the parking lot.

Glancing at his rear view mirror about 20 minutes into the trip Red counted the Sioux's car but no Crow. "Coward," he swore, "miserable Crow, cut an run, always." Sliding too fast into the Gardiner exit, Red felt his bald tires skate sideways through the turn. Keeping his foot off the brake, he managed to goose it with a little gas and straighten up. "Whoa pony, steady now." He coaxed the truck to a stop idling with the nose headed down hill just under the Blue Tongue Tavern's blinking sign. The final chorus of Proud Mary and the stomp of the cowboy two-step beckoned him as he got out of his vehicle and into the cold night. Tapping his foot to the beat on the crusted snow, he wondered if he had time to slip in for a quick one. But just as he headed for the door, the Sioux slid in spraying him with slushy mud. "Damn your red ass," he thundered pounding on the hood.

"Sorry man, didn't mean to," grinned Billy popping a beer, draining it in one long swallow and tossing the can in the back seat of his rusty pinto. Jake fiddled with the radio, searching for a signal.

Revving their engines against the cold, they agreed to meet at the game station located on the other side of town. Red proposed a toast to their bravery, but the Sioux were out of money and beer, so Red decided to hold on to his cache for his own ride back to the rez.

Cruising down the narrow, tree-lined lane toward the building, it began to occur to each of them that the only rig

that could hold any amount of meat was Red's pickup. Billy twisted around surveying the backseat of his pinto and cursed. Even if he removed all the beer cans, he and Jake each had a saddle to haul. And somehow, somewhere, they had picked up Kenny. Frozen buffalo weighed a lot and his rusty pony, short on pistons, couldn't pack much of a load.

The game station stood dark and deserted half-mile off the main street at the end of a long driveway. Originally a small warehouse, the metal building was fitted with a counter to sell and check hunting licenses, issue regulation pamphlets and maps and cold rooms to hang seized game and freezer lockers for longer storage.

"Two cars here now, somebody will notice. Load the meat in my truck, we can split it up down the road."

"I'm not trusting my share to Red," Billy said.

A large padlock secured the double-wide door. Red, checking the warehouse windows for an entrance, hollered over to Billy, "Suits me just fine asshole. I don't need to be hauling yours."

"Okay, okay, let's get this show on the road," Billy yelled. The beer had worn off along with his good humor leaving a heavy drum beat inside his head. Jake parked the car behind the building.

Walking around the metal building, the men checked each window for an opening. Clearly the padlock on the front door was a problem. "Shit-a-roo," exclaimed Red. "We are going to have to break out a window and hand the meat though that way. This lock is not gonna give," he said, kicking the front door with his cowboy boot.

"Shoot it off," offered Billy.

"Ya, right," Red said, "and let everybody in town know there is a raiding party."

"Psst!" Kenny poked his head out a window, hissing at them from inside the building. He was pulling on a joint, the fragrant weed pungent in the still night.

"How did you get in there?" said Jake.

"I am a spirit raven. Flew in," was the reply. Looking at him in astonishment, the men realized this was the first time the Cheyenne had spoken all night.

"Will you let us come in too?" said Jake.

"No," giggled the raven, "your spirits have flown the coup." His hysterical laughter echoed in the building.

"Hot damn," Red said, "we've got a crazy dope head to deal with now."

"Bring me a beer and I will reveal my secrets," suggested the raven, his blood shot eyes reflecting the moon's glow framed through the window. Everyone turned to Red, knowing he was the only one with that particular commodity.

Red clutched at his chest as if he was having a heart attack. It was painful to part with the last of his beer. Two cans left. He must not let the raven know.

"I'm out," he said lowering his bead.

"I say we shoot the lock off and plug the raven too while we are at it," snarled Billy. His head felt like a bronc was bucking his brains out.

The whoop - whoop of the raven echoed in the metal building.

"We have to shut him up," stated Billy, "and the only way I know is for you, Red, to give him one of those beers you are keeping from your brothers."

"Okay, I will check, maybe there is one I overlooked. Make him tell us how he got in first."

As Red was handing a beer through the window, Jake's face appeared next to the raven. "Give me one too and I will reveal the secret." Jake laughed by himself.

"What the hell," yelled Red. "I'm not givin' to no more crazy asses. How did you get in there?"

"I am the hawk," stated Jake, "about to get me a raven."

"Might just let that raven poop in his nest," muttered Red.

Without waiting for Jake to answer, Red tore around the corner of the building and right through the open side door, yelling, "I am the coyote and you are both dead fuckin' ducks."

Backing the truck up to the side door, the men loaded the buffalo that had been butchered in the field by Gabe, Paul and Leroy. The meat was tagged as evidence and had the Blackfeet tribal affiliation listed.

Dragging a cold, bloody robe through the hallway, Billy felt his Sioux Indian strength return. True, he had not ridden in the money. But that seemed so long ago when he had swallowed his pride chided by that Blackfeet gelding. Tonight he was a brave warrior riding a fierce stallion on a dangerous raid. He would bring home the spoils of this battle to his family. His wife would open her legs to him, his children would gather to hear his stories. Damn it, how he hated that the meat and this fine robe and his honor were being trusted to that Blackfeet dog.

Loading the last of the meat boxes in the back of the pickup, Billy slipped back inside the station for a last look. He really wanted that painting of the grizzly bear hanging there on the wall. Tracing the outline of the beast's hump and stretching his fingers to the mountain peaks surrounding the fierce animal, he thought about how nice it would look in his house. Put it by the stove and study it. Outside he could hear the truck tires spinning and sliding around on the icy driveway, the engine straining. Probably stuck. He'd have to walk out to his car anyway because there was no room in the pickup. Suddenly he became aware of the silence, then bright lights flashing through the windows and the sound of running. Tearing out the side door, Billy found himself looking down the black hole of a 357. The cop's shiny badge glistened in the moonlight. "Halt, there." The officer's voice held just a sliver of fear.

Young and scared, thought Billy. Edging slowly out the door with his hands above his head, he scanned the yard. Where is everybody? In the moonlight the truck, doors wide open, stood idling. A final cough and it quit.

The policeman's car, its strobe light fixed on the building, was parked sideways blocking the road exit. Not a trace of his friends and only one cop? Could be the other one was on the chase. Again Billy felt his Sioux strength pool swelling his

chest. Taking a step forward, he brought his fists down hard on the officer's forearm holding the pistol. A shot and Billy felt a burn inside his leg. With a roar, the rage of a century blanketed him like the shield of Crazy Horse. Reaching down, he locked his huge arms around the neck of the terrified officer and dragging him through the snow reached the police car. Snatching the keys from the ignition, he dragged the cop backwards, unlocked the trunk and shoved him in head first. Slamming the lid with a grin, he stepped back only to feel cold steel nudge him in the back of his head.

"Easy now, Injun boy, you'll be opening that trunk again and politely helping Officer Jeffries out of there." The voice was as icy and hard as the gun pointed at his brain. "Shit," thought Billy, nothin' scared about this one.

"Hot damn, they got my truck," Red's hoarse whisper sounded scratchy and too loud in the clear, cold night.

"They got Billy," whispered Jake tersely.

Hunkered down in the snow covered brush off to one side of the clearing, they squatted in the knee deep drifts shaking with cold as the alcohol left their blood stream headed for their bladders. Through the raw branches they could see Billy handcuffed and pushed into the patrol car. In the stiffening cold, the young officer's voice sounded edgy. "Should I stay with the pickup or bring the prisoner in?" The seasoned veteran paused and glanced around the clearing. "Let's both take him in. No place in town to keep him, have to take him to Bozeman. Don't want to leave just one of us out here, not knowing how many buddies Billy here has with him."

"I noticed a junker parked as we came through town," agreed the young officer.

"Grab the truck keys and let's go," the senior officer commanded climbing into the driver's seat.

Kenny hissed, "There is a car coming up the road." Dropping down, they watched as a dark pickup drove part way down the lane, stopped and made a U-turn rubbing up against the snow embankments on both sides.

"Who the hell was that?" said Red. "Probably that asshole Crow checking to see if his squealing worked. I say we hot wire and roll out." In less than five minutes they were moving down the lane headlights out. The windshield fogged over from three of them shoved in the cab. The meat was still in the pickup, but Billy's robe was nowhere.

Stopping next to Jake's car, they debated their next move. It was 4 AM and the spirits of both liquor and adventure had deserted them. "I can't make it back to Bozeman or much anywhere on what gas I have," said Red. "I say a visit to Crow Country? Damn betcha. I know where that traitor Pete lives. And it ain't but 20 miles from here. Be real glad to see us, I just know it."

##

Looking across the field at the sound of a holey muffler scratching the air, Pete saw a beat up Pinto, riding real low and a brown pickup with the Blackfeet Tribe insignia on the door, headed toward him. That asshole Red was leaning out the window of the truck waving and honking his horn.

"When you didn't show, we was afraid you got lost, so we come here to check on you," smirked Red, climbing out of the pickup all hunched over from gripping the steering wheel. The last ten miles had been sheer black ice and with the heavy load of frozen meat, he'd hit bottom in more ways than one. His head felt like rocks banging in a bucket. Party-time is way, long over he thought grimly.

From the door of the house, a heavy set woman watched in silence. Turning back inside, she slammed the door. "My auntie, she don't want no company. Uh, I don't either," said Pete.

Red shrugged. "We got no gas, wanna eat. Be a man, be a brother. You fix us up and we leave nice like."

"I got to sleep, even if it is beside a porky-pine like him," said Jake.

Pete glanced at the front door and back to Red. Pushing open the heavy log door, a blast of heat and the smell of meat frying hit Red, Jake and Kenny like a welcome mat. They made a beeline for the pot-belly stove.

Pete, his underwear sleeves shoved above his elbows, dropped more slabs of elk steak onto a smoking cast iron skillet. Turning the meat to brown on both sides with the tip of his skinning knife, he seemed oblivious to the grease splattering on his hands and arms. He had on his new cowboy hat from the rodeo.

"Slice some of this bread and toast it over the flames," he said tossing the loaf to Kenny. "You," he said pointing his knife at Jake, "turn them spuds there before they get any blacker and you," he nodded at Red, "scramble up some eggs." Pete was accustomed to cooking for hunters and always had food stockpiled especially during the winter. Red was wishing he hadn't goaded Pete into being a man. He was turning out to be a tough one.

Sitting around the long trestle table, the men bent their heads to the meal and ate quickly. The old woman sat in the corner and fixed them with black eyes that seemed to never blink. The only other sound was the soft scratching of a mongrel dog under the table hoping for a handout. Fried potatoes and onions, elk steak, brown–crisp, curled edges, red raw in the center, was a feast to the band. Finally, plates scraped clean,

Pete gathered up all the dishes and produced the makings to roll a cigarette. He offered it around but Jake and Red had store-bought brands. Kenny pulled on a plug of weed.

"Take it outside," Pete glared at him until he stubbed it out. "What brings you? You got trouble?" The smoke curling across his face didn't dim his level gaze.

Red slouched in his chair dozing. What with the heat, a full stomach and no sleep in 24 hours, he jerked upright knocking over his coffee cup. Pete tossed him the dishrag. Watching the brown puddle spread across the table, Red's thoughts jumbled. Damn cops, now a big mess to clean up.

"They owed us the meat. It just plain ain't right to keep it from hungry people. Them Feds think they control everything. But a man's belly will say different."

Pete waited, puffing on his home-rolled tobacco. He figured Red would talk until he dropped.

"We wound up in Gardiner last night about midnight, to liberate the buffalo butchered from the last Park kill. They were holding it to use against our brothers who were jailed trying to save a herd from some snowmobilers. You get the news out here, Pete?"

"Look on the roof. Satellite dish. Got a phone too. I heard about it. Your part hasn't come on yet."

"They got Billy," said Jake. "But he won't tell on us."

"Like hell, he won't," yelled Red.

"You shouldn't have riled him. He's big, he's tough. And you're just a weasel." Jake laughed quietly.

"I didn't get here alone," Red replied. "Pete," said Red, his eyes dull, "I don't plan real good when I've had too much beer and no sleep. Is there a place we can bed down for a couple of hours, then we figure it out?"

"There's bunkhouse out back with sleeping bags. I'll start a fire, it ain't had heat for a month or more," said Pete reaching for his jacket. "You gotta haul wood." For a minute, no one moved. Pete shrugged and tossed his jacket back on the chair and reached for the coffee pot.

At that, the weary crew struggled to their feet and filed out the door into the clear, cold morning. Jake lingered behind. Stepping into the bedroom off the kitchen he hurriedly dialed the telephone and in a hoarse whisper said, "Norma, listen woman, it may be longer still before I call again. We're headed for the back country. The Feds are coming for us. They got Billy. Gotta go."

## CHAPTER 4

# DARK MOON

Gabe pushed himself out from under the pickup, grease spotting his heavy parka. "Damn sled heads, it's their fault that it's gushing oil like an Arab bank account." He had driven all day from Yellowstone to Browning to deliver Old Man back to the reservation and away from trouble. Stopping long enough to grab a sleeping bag, snowshoes, food from home and his dog, Cisco, it was time to turn around and go get the meat. The carcasses had been lying in the field freezing for hours. He would be able to finish only the ones they had already skinned. Once the hide froze, it became impossible to separate it from the flesh. With the three of them cutting this morning it was to be at least a ten-hour job. Now, unless he could round up Leroy he'd have to go it alone. Nobody had heard from Paul all day. "Can't believe he would sit by that asshole's bedside. Maybe he's just waiting for me back at the site."

Dusk was just beginning to fold over the land like a pink velvet veil. Chief Mountain, a golden crimson, glistened with energy. Looking up at his birthright he thought about his life here and how it could all go away if the sledder dies. Could Old Man summon him good luck – call it a blessing – or was it to be always beyond his reach; denied because he didn't believe enough.

Nursing the nose of the truck through the snow drifts he headed out of his yard down the lane toward the interstate. Watching his taillights disappear, the horses leaned over the fence hoping for a pail of grain. But hay would have to hold them for a couple of days.

Chewing on a bologna sandwich, Gabe fiddled with the knobs on the radio. *"High winds, blowing snow warning for the east side of the Rockies,"* droned the announcer. Swinging onto the interstate, he slapped his thigh in time to the music singing along with Waylon and the boys, "Mama, don't let your babies grow up to be cowboys, let them be poachers and take out park rangers and such." Gabe liked to change the words to match his mood. He knew there was nothing better than being an Indian and a cowboy unless it was being him - a wildlife manager on the reservation. If he could just get a buffalo herd and the elk would stop getting shot up faster than they could drop a calf, people would be able to fill their bellies with meat not just government commodities. "How'd I get so lucky," he pondered. "A couple hundred acres, four walls and working outside all day. Now I just need me a faithful woman. One who is willing to wait until I am ready to settle down, but is full of good lovin' now." Gabe never lacked for female attention, but most of the time, the bother of moving it from flirting to fucking could be better spent hunting or fishing. "Now I just need one stupid sled head to live."

Keeping an eye on the oil gauge, he pushed the pedal hard. Rounding a corner, a gust of wind lifted the top off a snowdrift and dropped it on his windshield. The wipers plowed furiously. Peering through the dim light, he braked then swerved, sure he'd seen a deer standing in the middle of the highway. Blinking, he stared again and it was gone. "It's going to be a long night," he sighed.

The big semi-trucks roaring out of Canada hauling grain and logs half buried him with snow as they barreled past. The moon was covered with clouds cutting visibility. His headlights gave him just enough shine to keep driving but it was like being in a dimly lit tunnel. It was so black outside. How strange he thought that the farther south he drove, the closer he got to Yellowstone, the more he felt the cold creep into the truck cab. Usually Browning broke the records for low temperatures.

His bladder woke him. That and Cisco whining and gently nudging his face. Coming to with a start, he realized he was driving slowly down the shoulder of the road half in and out the ditch. But he had somehow managed to make the turn into the Park. Just ahead was the entrance gate welcoming all to *Yellowstone, America's First National Park.* Coming to a stop, he glanced at his watch and realized it was just before midnight. The last time he remembered checking, he had left the interstate for the two lane and it was closer to eleven. "Don't think I ever drove this long asleep before," he said chuckling to Cisco. "Lucky I didn't roll to the bottom of the canyon." Climbing stiffly out of the truck, he relived himself; the warm stream hissed hitting ice. Head cocked back he studied the black sky. The snow had stopped and the stars traced their legends. Through the pickup window he could hear the radio station ticking off the cattle and hog futures report, then with a flourish of sound effects announce a news breaking bulletin.

*"The state police and highway patrol urge you to be on the lookout for Gabriel Dumont. He is 32 years of age, five feet eleven inches, 180 pounds, with a mole on his right cheek. He has black hair worn in braids and brown eyes. Dumont is a member of the Blackfeet tribe and serves as their Fish and Game officer. He is wanted for questioning about his role in an incident in Yellowstone Park this morning where a snowmobiler was injured following a high speed chase while being pursued by Dumont, Paul Landry, director of the Blackfeet Head Start program in Browning and Leroy Little Coyote, a member of the Sioux tribe at Fort Peck. Two of the perpetrators are now in custody. The three tribal members were butchering the buffalo shot by the Park Service to take back to the reservations for*

*distribution when the incident occurred. Gabe Dumont has not been seen since approximately 9 AM. He is armed. He is driving a 2005 brown Chevrolet pickup with a Blackfeet Fish and Game emblem on the door. You are urged to exercise caution and report his whereabouts to the state patrol."* An ad selling snow machines followed the newscast.

Gabe stood there holding his limp dick. How had things moved so fast? Paul and Leroy in jail, the cops looking for his truck. What if that damn sled head dies.

Climbing back into the warm cab, he sat there weighing his choices. They'd be looking for him in Browning. Better keep going. "Jesus," he thought, "here I am back here. How stupid is that. Then again, maybe not." His thoughts raced. "I need someplace to think this through, see if the dumb shit dies and go from there." Ticking off his supply list, he had a rifle, a skinning knife, some matches, a sleeping bag, snowshoes and some food to last for a couple of days. Lots of buffalo meat just waiting.

He was glad there wasn't anybody sitting at home waiting and crying her eyes out. Course there was the horses, but they would be okay for a couple of days. His mother and father had both passed away leaving just him. His cousin, Red, was riding in the Bozeman rodeo, not far from here. Probably back in Browning by now.

Thoughts of Red before he was such an asshole, reminded him of a hot springs site they used to go to here when they were kids exploring Yellowstone with their grandfathers. It was about ten miles in from the gate and a quarter mile or so off the road, not all that far from the butchering site. It shouldn't be visible by anyone driving by unless they were looking hard. Thermal water bubbled out of a shallow cave big enough to break the wind and the snow. It was warm too. No front door though, grinned Gabe wryly. He might be sharing quarters with a grizzly looking for a place to bed down.

Sitting in his truck gazing at the Welcome to Yellowstone National Park sign, he pondered his next move. He wanted – he needed – some of that buffalo meat they had left at the butchering site. Seemed really unlikely that anyone would be around at this hour. But, then, if they were, while they couldn't see him, he couldn't see them either. Better get his butt out of here and out of sight. Come back when it was lighter and check things out.

Gabe nosed the rig around the signposts. If this were a movie instead of his fucked up life, he thought wryly, he would simply shoot the lock off, cowboy style.

He hoped it would snow before daylight and cover his tracks. Snow machine ruts lined the road, so even if it didn't, he'd probably be okay he thought. For once, he was content to follow in the path of the noisy, ugly machines.

Now, where was that turn off to get to the cave? Glancing at his gas gauge, he hoped he found it on the first try. Should have filled up in Gardiner. Talk about being asleep at the wheel.

"Shit, it is black out here." The clouds had moved in hiding the stars. The moon was wearing a hazy hood. The road curved through the trees, his headlights showing only match thin blackened trunks. The fires of '88 had burned through here. Beside him, Cisco whined and nudged his arm. "You mongrel, why didn't you pee when we were already stopped. Just like a damn kid." Braking the pickup, he leaned over and opened the door, the dog jumped out and lifted his leg against the tire. A minute later, Cisco barked and took off through the underbrush.

"Oh shit, you know better." Jumping out of the truck he yelled, "Cisco, get your black ass back here. You go chasing something bigger than you and you'll end up supper." Lighting a cigarette, he leaned against the warm hood, the vibration of the motor lulling his tired body. "Spotting this cave at night may not be one of my better ideas," he thought. It had been over twenty years since the last time he and Red had been out here. Still, he prided himself on never feeling lost and could always return to a place. But it was close to 2 a.m. and his butt was dragging and now Cisco was on a hunting party. "Maybe I'll just take a little nap." Pulling the sleeping bag out, he stretched it out across the seat and turned off the engine. Settling down, he had just dozed off when he felt the truck begin to gently rock. Raising his head slowly, he could just make out a large hairy rump with a swishing tail. Every time it sashayed and rubbed up against the warm hood, the rear-view mirror bent a little more. With a snap, it hit the frozen ground startling the moose who backed up, shook his head and pawed the ground ready for the charge. Gabe could hear Cisco growl from under

the truck. “Oh great, this is all I need. Oh my aching ass.” 

Opening the door, he yelled, “Cisco, get your hide in here. Moose, take it on down the road.” Obediently the dog slithered out from under the truck and leapt onto the cab floor. The moose shook its great head and turned toward the trees; and with a shake of its antlers, the big guy disappeared into the brush. Gabe crawled back in his bag.

By six a.m. Gabe was awake and feeding his engine the last of the oil to slow the hemorrhaging. Reluctantly the cold starter turned over and with a puff of blue smoke, the truck creaked slowly down the frozen path. His tires thumped like rocks every time they hit the flat spot from being parked. Cisco shivered on the seat beside him.

Peering through the dim light, he could just make out the familiar shelf of rock, the bench marking the spot above the cave. Turning off the path, he knew it was time to hide the pickup. Driving any closer wasn’t an option with the downed timber. He’d have to hoof it packing supplies. Loading a tarp with gear, he figured to drag it, cover his tracks. For the moment, it felt great to be out here in the silent cold, free, nowhere to go. Maybe nowhere to go but down he thought angrily.

## CHAPTER 5

# SHUDDA MY MOUTH

She stared at him through the bars, her long black hair shadowing her expression. Seeing her, he felt the familiar pain in his heart, the longing that never dimmed. She held his gaze for a moment, then, lowering her eyes, she said quietly, "I've come to get you out, posted bail."

"Why you? Red actually let you come? Where's Gabe? Did they get him too?" Paul's initial relief flipped to the immediate.

"Let's talk in the car. This place scares me," she whispered.

Checking his belongings, Paul stepped into the early light grateful for the fresh morning smell. Jail stunk in more ways than one. Lucy waited, the engine running.

"Paul, what is going on, I haven't seen nor heard from Red since he left for the Bozeman rodeo three days ago. He was supposed to meet me here in Billings last night after my conference." Lucy's slight frame drew tight clutching the steering wheel like it was a life preserver. "Mama called, said the cops came to the house looking for him and Gabe. She told me she heard about you on the news." Catching him with a sideways glance, she said, "It's lucky for you I was down here, or you, buddy, would still be in the tank."

"Appreciate the bail. I'll get it back to you. I know why they want to see Gabe, but what's Red got going? He wasn't with us. Do you know where Leroy is?"

"He's still here, they are planning to hold him longer because of his prison record. I saw him this morning and he was still stinking drunk from the night before," sighed Lucy. "He must have really tied one on. They are also holding a Sioux, big guy, name of Billy. As for Red, you tell me. I just hope he's okay," her voice caught an edge.

"I know nothing about nobody. Your hot shot boyfriend can find his own trouble. I've got plenty of my own to worry about."

"Paul, don't let your feelings about Red make you mean. This Billy claims Red was with him and they tried to get the meat back from the federal game station at Gardiner. Said Red run out on him. Mama also got the idea from the cop that Red is somehow mixed up in your mess."

"I don't see how, said Paul bitterly. "Big Red was in Bozo riding for the big money and the big buckle for only him and maybe to impress you. He's not interested in helping feed the people on the rez."

"Your truck is parked over there," said Lucy with a jerk of her head, her eyes boring holes in the windshield.

"Hey, woman o'mine, I'm just a jerk," Paul said touching her cheek, "but he is so bad for you."

Lucy jerked away. "Paul, let it go. You left me, remember."

Paul opened the door and stepped out. Without a glance, Lucy shifted into reverse and backed the car out of the lot and into the traffic.

Watching her drive away, he wished he could make her see that he needed to go before he could really be here. I didn't know what it was to be Indian till I left. I've come back to do some good. But why can't I learn to shut my mouth about Red he thought grimly kicking the snow off the tail lights. Spotting a phone booth, he decided to call Old Man and find out about Gabe. Hunched over in the cold waiting for an answer he pondered her remark. Get the meat back? What was that asshole Red up to?

CHAPTER 6

# HOTPOTS & POT HEADS

"It's lookin' to noon," yelled Pete, throwing open the bunk house door. "You boys better start looking at something beside the backside of your eyeballs." Striding from bunk to bunk, he nudged them with the tip of his boot to their butts. "You are all over the news. Seems your buddy Billy is lonely in jail without you."

"What did I tell you," yelled Red, "that whiny bastard turned on us. No Blackfeet can trust a Sioux, never could."

"Hold on, you woman beatin'- horse snatchin', miserable half-breed," yelled Jake springing from the bunk and grabbing Red by the foot of his sleeping bag. Red hit the floor with a thud. Struggling to free himself from the bag wrapped around him like a moth in a cocoon, Red screamed, "You dog humpin'…"

"Whoa, save your energy for the real enemy," said Pete grabbing the back of Jake's shirt, ducking as Jake spun around, his fist looking for a place to land.

All that could be seen of Kenny was braids snaking across the pillow.

"There are going to be Feds fanning every road around Gardiner. I don't need it here. Get up. Get goin'."

Once again, Red wished he hadn't encouraged Pete's manliness. It was getting old.

Hastily the men dressed while Pete, arms crossed like a drill Sargent, barked out questions. Where were they headed?

What were they going to need to get there? The only thing the reluctant warriors wanted to do was take their hangover home. "Too late for that," said Pete. "Should have thought of that before you played coup at the game station. The Feds don't like it when the Indians pull a fast one on their land."

The men filed into the dimly lit storage room amid the rich smell of leather saddles and tack lining the walls, wool blankets and feather down-filled sleeping bags and boxes of smoke singed cookware. Gear to take on an adventure, a trip, an escape.

Red stuck out his pointy cowboy boot. "There is nothing I would rather wear than my Tonys unless it's packing in the mountains in the winter. Got some snow boots Pete?"

"I got two pairs. The last time I counted you bunch there

were three. Most fools don't come up here without foot gear. Guess you better draw straws or wrestle."

"Where are we going to go," said Kenny, "whose name did they say on the radio?"

"They had Red's name down for real. I didn't catch the whole report."

"Billy squealed," Red spit the words.

"Like hell he did," retorted Jake. "They took your license plate number."

"Red, I'm thinking I better go back to Bozeman." Kenny stood in the shadows, his voice muffled. "My woman, she's alone with the cows. The horses are turned out and there is much snow."

"You bailing? You takin' a fade on me Kenny?" Red closed the distance between them.

Kenny, head level with the pockets on Red's shirt, nose almost touching, shifted only his eyes scanning the room like a nervous Spaniel.

"There are many coming to my place for a sweat ceremony tomorrow," he continued, his voice barely audible. "I got to build the fire in the lodge, heat the rocks and make the soup. Prepare myself with fasting and prayer."

"Kenny, the only thing you have to prepare yourself for is another night in the drunk tank," said Red. "You ain't got no home, no woman, for damn sure, no cows or horses. You're staying, till we get this figured out. Red don't want you out there blabbin' your mouth.

"When you runnin' out?" challenged Red, staring at Jake.

Jake tossed a frying pan in the pile and said, "I ain't. They got Billy. That leads to me. But I ain't so damn sure I'm going anywhere with the likes of you."

"Who invited ya. Blood can run thin when the cops start closing in," sneered Red. "Just how did the cops know who piked the meat. I'm thinking ole Red will head into the Park for a few days," said Red. "Just let things cool off, see what comes down with Billy. No jail for this Injun."

"You are one dumb sucker, they traced your name off your plates," snarled Jake.

"You are just so damn sure about that, but guess what, that truck ain't registered in my name on account that I got a

couple of bad tickets off the rez that I didn't pay so that truck technically belongs to the tribe," said Red, his voice flat. "I got my cousin to list it on the rolls. If you look real close, it's a government plate." His hooded eyes glinted in the dimly lit room like a bull snake coming out of his hole.

"Billy is not going to tell and risk my hide," mumbled Jake. "If he turns you in, he nails me.  He won't do it."

"What about that Crow that flew the coop," asked Kenny. "He might be blabbing."

"Kenny, guess you forgot, we're guests in 'that Crow's' place. Ya know, the guy who fed us."

"Oh ya," mumbled Kenny

"Guys, like I said, you ain't got all day to get even. You need to get goin'. Just exactly what do you have in mind besides a stroll in the Park on this fine ass-freezing day."

"I'm still thinking the Park. Can't go back to Browning, for damn sure," said Red. "Go on private property and some hothead rancher will shoot us for trespassing. Head into the Park, find a nice hot springs, eat some of this meat I been packing around and wait."

"Get this gear back here in a week or I am coming to get it and your ass," said Pete.

Crowded in the pickup, Kenny in the middle, the three men drove in uneasy silence. Red and Jake both knew the temporary truce forged out of necessity was fragile.

"Who'd believe," mused Jake, "24 hours ago we were shaking our brains up straddling a bucking bronc."

"Looks to me," replied Red, "like we still are. Only this time there is no out rider to pick you up when you get throwed."

Kenny pulled out a reefer. In a moment, the sweet arid smoke filled the cab.

"You crazy bastard snub that out. You want us dead in the ditch before we even hit the Park," yelled Red. "I am all for a good time, but man, I don't need no funny weed to screw with me right now."

"Okay, okay. Stay cool man," murmured Kenny. "Just a little sweet grass."

"Sweet grass, my ass," exploded Red. "I know Maryjane when I smells it you pothead."

The afternoon sun was just setting on the tree tops when they crossed the Park entrance. Would be dark within an hour.

The only traffic they met were rigs pulling snow machine trailers headed out. No state patrol or rangers in sight.

Driving slowly down the rutted road, they scanned the country looking for the tell-tale plume of steam that meant hot springs. Like their ancestors before them, if the snow got too deep, the tribe would move further in, find a hotpot and bask in the waters. The Park had always been considered sacred ground belonging to all tribes. No warfare was tolerated. The buffalo and elk also migrated to these areas where they didn't have to fight the drifts. They too would bask in the hot mud. Nature's spa. Hunting became a task no more difficult than stepping outside the tipi, as easy as selecting meat from the case at Safeway.

Bouncing along in the hot truck cab, Jake finally exploded. "Let me the hell out of here. Kenny stinks. It's too damn close in here. I'll camp any place just to get some air."

Red just kept driving, watching the horizon. Sure enough, soon they glimpsed a wisp of vapor trailing across the tundra like a mare's tail cloud. Keeping a watch while they drove looking for a pull out, they suddenly realized that the cloud moved in a direct line. It was not white, but more blue and hazy. "It's one them miserable sled heads," yelled Red. "Never liked those skunk wagons."

"Hey man, we better get to gettin' a place to camp," said Jake, "I don't want to be wandering around in the dark and fall into some hotpot."

"Looks to me like Hardrock Hotel coming right up," said

Red. Pulling the pickup off on the shoulder, they felt the back end slide off the hard-pack into the soft ditch. Sighing, Kenny and Jake climbed out. Bracing themselves, they pushed the thrashing truck out of the hole back on the road.

Trudging toward the hotpot, they looked for places to camp, shelter from the cold wind and concealment from the road. Snow clung to tuffs of grass on the wind-blown volcano bone yard. Stumbling over the uneven ground pockmarked by hardened lava deposits plopped like so many cow pies across the prairie, they scanned the horizon. Closer to the pot, there was nothing but a thicket of willow surrounded by lodge-pole pine burned black and limb-less from the '88 fires. Petrified trees stacked like cord-wood lined up behind the pot. Picking their way carefully, they reminded each other that they were literally treading on thin ground. With every step they risked breaking through the shale crust and ending up being the protein in 200-degree pea soup.

"You call this a camp spot," sneered Jake. "Tell me again, why the hell do we need this hotpot anyway? I'm in no mood to hear stories about the old hunting days and I'm not crazy about wandering around out here, end up falling in some damn hole and getting boiled."

"You want to camp in three feet of snow," Red shot back. "How are we going to cook the buffalo tonight? It's frozen solid. Where are you planning to find dry wood, nature boy? If you use your head and watch your step the only thing boiled will be our dinner."

Kenny stumbled along behind giggling, dragging the gear bag with the sleeping bags and pulling on a joint.

Tying a tarp between two trees, the men made a makeshift wind break. Carving into the frozen meat, Jake fashioned a rope like a sling around a fat rump roast and was about to lower it into the boiling cauldron, when Red yelled.

"You want it to taste like rotten eggs," Red flashed, "just like it smells out here. Put it in this pot Pete lent us, throw in some onions and rest the pot on the edge in the shallow part. The water is boiling, I think it will cook just fine. Gotta teach you everything," he added with a sneer.

Settling down deep in their bags they listened to the owl perched on a snag jutting out of the petrified logs above their heads.

"The owl is a shadow across the moon," said Kenny softly. "He is a messenger of bad things to come. Maybe if I am very quiet, be real small like a rabbit in a hole, he won't come for me."

"Oh hell Kenny," laughed Red, "you'd be slim pickens for a Magpie so don't be puffin yourself."

"Maybe he wants a bigger slab like you Red," Kenny snickered.

"Just maybe, you better shut your mouth," said Red.

Night, quiet like a blanket pulled over, settled across them. The only sound was the percolating, gurgling, bubbling, mud pots.

"Do these things ever blow up?" asked Jake.

"Yup. Don't sleep too close," replied Red.

"I remember the stories the old guys tell about this place," said Jake, "but to me, it's not sacred ground, it's scary ground. A fissure could open up and swallow us. Anytime now. Just like that," he said clicking his fingers.

"Would you can it, I'm trying to sleep here," snarled Red.

Lying there breathing in the sulfur air and debating whether to get up and reposition his bag to better fit the slope of the hard ground, Red had a sudden thought. "Hot damn," he exclaimed sitting upright in his bag. "I know a place! Old Man and my grandfather used to take me and Gabe to some caves near here. We slept there many a night. Gabe might even be there unless he took to the mountains behind his Browning place."

"Can we just stay put and get some sleep first. I am not going to cross this hell-hole in the dark," moaned Jake.

"Great, first you bitch about being here, now I can't get you to leave, just like an old woman," sneered Red. "Okay, we head out in the morning. So shut up and sleep."

"I gotta pee," whined Kenny.

CHAPTER 7

# GIVE US OUR MEAT

Paul cradled the telephone between his ear and shoulder and plugged coins into the telephone. No answer at Gabe's. Who else could he call? Old Man had a phone, but he rarely picked it up. His daughter paid the bill every month and hoped that if he had any trouble he'd use it.

Old Man shouted back into the receiver. "Very cold, blizzard, big winds, power go off sometimes, can't talk, gotta go." Old Man had driven in to Browning that morning over to the senior center to wait for the meat truck. The Park Service had finally agreed to release some of the buffalo meat to the tribe. There were many hungry people this winter with the game being scarce.

Some of the Traditionalists had agreed amongst themselves

not to touch the meat as the Park Service had finished the butchering and wrapping in a meat plant, without ceremony, without honor, without their help.

Pushing open the frost-covered door to the Center that morning, Old Man could hear the low voices of the Traditionalists discussing the situation. Standing nearby, a young woman rocking a baby with her small son clutching her leg, was demanding meat.

"I need it. My husband, he's gone. I don't know where. We are hungry," her plaintiff plea turned into a wail. Her little boy slumped to the floor at her feet and began to sob.

"The Feds have turned the buffalo into rations now, a 'commod,' treated no better than macaroni," muttered an ancient one. His tiny frame was wrapped in an tattered floral bedspread. Eyes dimmed by cataracts, he peered out the window at the blizzard as though through a veil seeing past the room, the dead cactus in the window, howling wind, the misery. "These are hard times."

Outside, the Park Service panel truck idled in the parking lot. The young rangers blasted the heater and the radio, scrapped at the frost on the windshield and waited. They were told by their supervisors to unload the meat and let the elders determine the distribution. But when they carried the first boxes to the kitchen door they were stopped by a line of old people. Their slumped, stooped bodies leaned in all directions like an old pole fence ready to collapse but braced in place by will. The rangers retreated to their van and called headquarters.

Old Man poured a thin cup of coffee, added three sugars and a packet of powered cream. His hands thawed some by the warmth. He joined the group gathered around the oil stove. The heat came in waves buffeted by a cold blast each time the door opened as more hunger filed in hugging the walls, wiping the last stale crumbs from the cookie box, draining the coffee pot. The room's three chairs and a spring-sprung sofa held people squeezed tight.

"The Creator will see it this way," argued Old Man. "Rules that hurt people, starve them, are the white man's invention. We all learned the good way from our elders, but these are hard, hard times," he punctuated his words with his fingers striking his heart.

"The government has violated the buffalo spirit," retorted one of the elders. "The meat will sicken us. It is probably already rotten."

"Are we to haul fresh-kill buffalo to the dump," pleaded Old Man. "Leave it to stink in the front yard? Where is the respect in that?"

"It is our way."

"You can afford to call upon the old ways." Old Man's voice steeled. "You have a herd of fat black Angus on your place. The people who come here today, through a blizzard, come because they don't have your steaks sizzling on a platter. These are your people, your family. They got nothin'. Buffalo meat nourishes, renews the spirit, brings hope."

Slowly the nods grew around the circle. At the hope, the

people lining the walls, straddling kitchen chairs, thin shoulders squeezed close in the drafty room stood a little straighter and with a side-ways glance, agreed.

Outside in the van, the rangers watched the gas gauge, their passage home, dip below half. "Let's get the hell out of here. They don't want this meat, it's fine by me," growled the driver shifting into reverse.

"We can't haul this load all the way back to Great Falls," said his partner. "We don't have enough gas. I say we stack it by the kitchen door. They can do with it as they damn well please.  We've done our part."

Jerking open their doors, they were surprised to see a windbreak of people standing stoically in the blowing snow stretching from the Senior Center kitchen door to the back of their van.

"Give us our meat."

## CHAPTER 8

# ONCE DOMESTIC, GONE WILD

Gabe tucked the last branch in the front of the cave hiding his pickup. "Probably freeze up and I won't get it started till spring," he muttered. "Ain't going far anyway, low on gas, low on oil, low on go."

The area was a labyrinth of caves, big ones with hot springs flowing through the center, small twisted ones where a badger had to crawl in backwards with no room to turn around. Sulfur fumes hung over the area like a cosmic fart. He chose the one with a fresh water stream which emptied into a small open cauldron before leaving the cave. "Pretty deluxe, both hot and cold running water," he said to himself. Stripping naked, he squatted where hot met cold and lathered himself. Shivering in the early morning, copper skin all goose bumps, he thought about the times he had spent here with his father and grandfather. Every morning, till the day he died, his father, drunk or sober, had bathed in the river. Sometimes breaking a hole in the ice. Then he would greet the rising sun with thanksgiving prayers to the creator. He was a gentle man who tried to protect his son from the crazed woman who was his mother. Gabe couldn't understand how his father could believe in goodness with so much badness around them. Ritual did not protect them. Gabe felt a pain squeeze his heart. He wished they could still be together at the campfire, telling the stories. Could Father hear him from the other side? Striking his breast with his palm he felt a warm breath on his cheek. For a moment a familiar blanket folded around him, the air thickened with the scent of sweet grass.

Tying his shiny braids with a leather thong, he stiffened as Cisco awoke with a growl and leapt toward the front of the cave. Five feet away, a tall, lean woman stood framed in the opening. Her startled eyes scanned the dim light in the cave finally focusing on him. Slowly she raised her rifle. "Hey you! Buck naked," her surprise overshadowed her fear.

Grabbing his sleeping bag, he attempted to cover himself while keeping an eye on her rifle.

"Hey woman, careful with that firearm, I don't want you to get nervous and shoot off something important."

"Hey, Indian boy, why should I be nervous, I'm not standing here bare ass. I'm the one with the gun." Her throaty laugh sounded like she had just smoked a carton of Camels.

"Look out behind you," shouted Gabe as he leapt the distance and grabbed the rifle as she swung around to look.

Staring into her eyes, he detected more provocation than fear. This was no young fawn. Age and experience etched her face, hardened her challenge. In a flash she snatched the rifle back. He was so surprised that for a moment he just stood there, then reaching out, he grabbed her in a bear hug, wretched the rifle from her and threw it over his shoulder. The discharge exploded echoing off the walls. The blast so startled them they instinctively clutched each other. Standing in embrace, he

forgot his embarrassment and felt only the warm thrust of her hips pressed to his. In the next second, he was on the ground, clutching his groin.

"You arrogant bitch, you kneed me," he moaned.

"You are awfully mouthy for somebody in your position. You look silly too." She laughed nudging him with her boot.

For a second, he thought about grabbing her leg and wrestling her to the ground, but he felt sure he'd end up on the short end.

"I'm guessing you are not related to Sitting Bull, more like lying gopher. What the hell are you doing here? This is my land. I could shoot you for trespassing," she said stepping over him to grab her rifle.

"This is Yellowstone, lady, it belongs to the people.

Especially Indian people," he added.

"Sorry, buster, but a year back my family inherited the old Silver Ridge ranch which has been a part of this park since before it was a park and this cave goes with it," she added with a smirk. "You may be a native, but you still look like a poacher to me."

"Could you wait outside while I get dressed? It is January after all."

"Oh, ya right, I am going to wait outside while you find your ammo, get your sorry act together and come blazing out of the cave on the warpath. Do I look like I fell out of the back of a pinto? Besides, why be modest now, I have seen you from every angle and I got to say, you are well hung together."

Gabe felt his face burn. He was just not used to women being so direct. "No woman should be talking to a man this way," he growled.

"No Indian woman would darlin', but I am not of your tribe. Although my kind has been messing around with yours since the days of the trappers."

"Why don't you step out of your duds and let me get a look at you," he sneered.

"You ain't climbing on me," she retorted. "Get your clothes on before my foreman, Two Bits, comes looking for me."

Lying there, his groin aching, his stomach churning, he thought for a moment about just asking her to put him out of his misery. Things just kept going from bad to worse.

"Take a deep breath, you'll be fine," she said softly.

"Oh, you have some experience in this, do you? Next time I crowd you a little, how about a plain old nod, or a nudge. I could even take a 'go to hell'."

"Next time?" she laughed, "Are you planning to turn this into a life-time deal, chatting over the fence, drinking at the bar? You, boy, need to go back to the reservation or wherever in the hell you came from. By the way, what did you ride in on? The only thing I hate more than poachers are snow machine jerks."

"I ain't no boy and maybe we got something in common," said Gabe. "Sled heads are at the top of my shit list alongside mouthy women," he snickered. Pulling himself up, he tried to casually pull his jeans on. It was a tossup which ached worse, his groin or his pride.

"Don't you wear underwear?" she asked, arching her brow. Squatting by the fire, she helped herself to the coffee with his mug while he dressed.

"Not always," his mocking eyes raked her as he slowly tucked his shirt into his jeans and zipped.

As he reached for his boots, she cautioned, "Move real slow, I would hate to have to shoot such a specimen."

"Why don't I believe that," he said grinning.

"What are you doing here, are you hiding out. Did you kill someone?" Her frankness disarmed him.

"Yes, I'm sorta hiding. And no, I did not kill anybody. The dumb son-of-a bitch may die, but he did it to himself."

"Maybe you should tell me about that part – the part that makes him guilty as hell – and you an innocent bystander," she said spitting coffee grounds in the bubbling pool.

"Is your foreman really likely to show up, or is that bullshit? Besides, Two Bits? Come on, that's a cartoon, bad movie name."

"Let me put it this way, do you think my Old Man is going to let me wander around for hours without somebody checking on me?" She sipped his coffee, her eyes always watching, scanning him, then a quick glance toward the entry. "Are you alone, cause unless he's on my side, I will blast the next one who comes through that hole."

"Lady, what is your problem. Why the tough ass routine? Can you keep from kicking or shooting me for a minute so we can just sit here like two human beings and discuss this?"

"Sure, after all, it is your coffee I'm drinking. Sit across, keep your hands where I can see them and we will have a lovely little chat," she drawled, "while I help myself to coffee and a cookie," she said, grabbing a bag of cookies out of the food box. "By the way, my name is Feral. You can call me Ms. Feral."

"Feral. That name just figures. Once domesticated gone wild," said Gabe. "There is only one cup, Ms. Feral," he said dragging on the Mss.

"We'll share, but right now, it's still my turn. Besides, I never did get the hang of being domesticated, just the gone wild part."

"Things are really messed up," he said staring into the

space above her head. "We were butchering buffalo shot by the park rangers to feed our people back on the rez when some snowmobilers showed up and decided to run a herd to death. We tried to stop them, one of the idiots ran his machine over the other, but I swear I didn't cause that."

"Oh, ya," she said nodding, "now I know who you are. You've got to be Gabe somebody, Blackfeet Fish and Game warden, right? You are all over the news, big time, honey."

"Shit." Gabe inhaled sharply.

"Yup. What do you bet they nail you with at least manslaughter if that guy dies," she nodded slowly. "But you did the right thing. I hate what snowmobilers do to the wildlife in the Park and what the Feds call managing the buffalo issue is just another word for wholesale slaughter. It sucks. But you know how the ranchers in this area feel about buffalo infecting cattle."

"Is your husband one of those scared ranchers?"

"I don't have a husband," she said frowning. "My stubborn, old as dirt dad, is definitely not on the side of the buffalo. But then he doesn't agree with the federal plan either. Actually it is hard to imagine him agreeing with anything or anybody. Back to you now, what is your plan? Surely this isn't the best you can do."

"Don't bother me I'm thinking," he said snatching the cup from her hand and draining the dregs.

##

Punching the gas, the truck slid sideways, hit the snow

bank, swapped ends and bounced back on the road headed back the way they came.

"Better be seeing that as a message," cautioned Kenny, "from Napi the coyote, the trickster, coming to play with our spirits."

"Napi my ass," exclaimed Red. "Ole Red will skin his hide and stretch it across the hood." Glancing over, he snickered at the horrified look on his two companion's faces. "Oh come on, Napi likes a good joke, he knows we're foolin' around."

"With you talking like that we are so screwed," whispered Kenny. "Might as well gut myself right here. Napi will fix us for sure."

Pulling off the road, Red motioned toward a rise on horizon. "The cave is that way. Grab your gear."

Plodding through the thicket they heard the underbrush rustle. Coming to a halt, Jake and Kenny close behind, Red knelt down and steadied his rifle. Pulling up sharply, he was knocked backward as Cisco leapt from the bush, licked Red's face, whimpering his joy.

Laughing, Red pushed the frantic dog off his chest and grabbing him by his collar, commanded the dog to sit and take them to Gabe. Cisco sat in the middle of the trail looking quizzical cocking his head from side to side.

"I would guess the dog doesn't know whether to sit or go." Jake leaned against a tree smoking a cigarette. Kenny sat in the wet snow, rocking back and forth, humming a mindless tune.

Patting Cisco on the head, Red commanded, "Go Cisco, find Gabe."

Hearing voices outside the entrance of the cave, Gabe and Feral moved to the shadows, one to each side of the door flat against the side.

Peering into the dimness, Red hollered out, "Hey Gabe, you in there, buddy, it's me."

Watching the three file into the cave, where Gabe and Red greeted each other with a nod while Cisco leapt in circles of joy, Feral shook her head and said, "What the hell is this, an open house. What kind of lame hiding place is on everybody's social stroll."

CHAPTER 9

# THE PLIGHT OF THE MAGPIE

Despite the fact that the Park Service continued to butcher and package in a plant, Paul, out on bail with two days before his hearing and three-day-old clothes, decided to high-tail it back into Browning. He needed to check on his place and arrange for someone to fill in for him at the school. He hoped Old Man could tell him where Gabe was. He'd go out to the place and check on the horses. By now, Lucy had probably figured out Red's disappearance. He was probably shacked up somewhere with a babe and a bottle.

The highway stretched like a shiny black ribbon – cold,

long and lonely. It seemed to go on forever across the prairie. The wind had scoured bare the tops of the snowy undulating hills, their crowns tipped with the brown of winter kill grass. It reminded him of a landscape of breasts poking the horizon. Then of Lucy. But the milk has turned, curdled, he thought with great weariness. He had come back to Montana, to his tribe, with such hope and expectation. This constant struggle with the Feds over land, buffalo, money and resources that rightfully belonged to the original people, was taking everyone's energy.

By early afternoon he had gassed up in Great Falls, grabbed a burger and was headed toward Browning three hours north. Waiting for his sandwich to thaw in the microwave at the quick-stop store while he got fuel, he caught part of a broadcast about the starving buffalo continuing to leave the park. The rangers were complying with the policy demands that they be shot, but they weren't calling in the tribes to butcher as they had been. As one reporter stated, *"Until the potential manslaughter situation has been fully investigated and the extent to which the tribes are involved is known, the program is halted."* He listed the snowmobiler's condition as still critical in intensive care in Billings. Paul considered asking the cashier if he had heard anything about Gabe, but decided against calling attention to himself.

The farther north he drove the worst the wind blew. Snowfall fell at an angle. Headlights made halos and ghostly shapes without edges. This was winter at the foot of Chief

Mountain. Many winters, families stranded miles from town would be close to eating their dogs before the snowplow could clear the roads and bring them supplies. Horses and cattle were turned out in the fall to fend for themselves. It would be spring before the livestock loss would be known. Charlie Russell, the cowboy artist, told stories of the winter of 1886-87 when ranchers could walk for 50 miles in any direction on the backs of their dead cattle. This had the makings of one of those terrible years.

Pulling into Old Man's driveway, he knocked on the heavy wood door. Like Old Man himself, the log house was lilting a little to the left, but could withstand many more blizzards. After a minute cold overcame politeness. Pushing open the door, Paul was hit by a blast of heat from the wood stove.

Sweet strains of an old Metis fiddle tune floated across the room. Old Man sat by the stove on a straight back chair, his gnarled hands gently plucked the strings and caressed them with his bow. His eyes were closed in remembrance of the good times his father had told him about when his French/ Indian relatives would come down from Canada pulling their Red River carts piled high with buffalo robes to trade. Sashaying bright as peacocks he could still see the men in their long capote coats made from stripped Hudson Bay blankets. They wore fur hats and tall leather moccasins and a woven, multi-color sash wrapped around their waists, just as their fathers and grandfathers had worn. The women were like the mud wren, plain, blending into the landscape safe from notice. The 1885 Riel Rebellion had stripped the peacock of its feathers. And now, a hundred winters later, even his cousins rarely crossed the border.

But more and more it was the music that Old Man could still see – stay up all night, play the homemade fiddles for hours, shuffling your feet to the jigs cause you just couldn't keep still. Folks used to say that the Metis had the craziness of the French and the craftiness of the Indians. Old Man knew they lived in the two worlds and were adrift in both. Now there were only the tunes to remember the stories that played in his mind.

Paul poured himself a cup of the coffee from the pot simmering on the back of the wood stove. It was thick as crankcase oil. Three sugars, a dollop of canned milk and he could maybe ease it past his nose for a quick swallow.

Pulling up a chair and sitting across from Old Man, Paul waited. Old Man, eyes still closed, played notes and chords and parts of half-remembered runs. Crossing the floor for more coffee, the music invited Paul to find his place in the rhythm. His feet began to shuffle, toe, heel, step, step. He danced in a circle with Old Man at the center. The moon peeked at him from each window as he spun past. After a time, the fiddler got to his feet and fell in step with him, the music weaving through, carried in them. The songs spoke of being alone, scared and hungry.

Hungry for freedom while searching for home. A worn out dog lying singe-close to the stove opened one eye, yawned and dozed off from the effort.

Finally, the moon slipped behind the mountain and the room turned dark. Paul crawled up next to the dog wrapping himself in the buffalo robe spread on the floor. Too soon he felt the nudge of Old Man's foot against his back. "We go to the sweat lodge. Purify ourselves. Many prayers to offer. Much help is needed."

Groggy from turning on the hard floor all night, Paul decided that the only praying he was going to do was from his Sears and Roebuck mattress and a heavy quilt with no smelly dog. Sleep until noon. It was still dark out. But Paul struggled to his feet. "Do you know where Gabe went?" he said.

"Yes," replied Old Man. "I know these things."

"Where?"

"We must pray first, sweat, then bathe in the river."

"I need to figure out what to do, we have some serious problems. I could end up in jail."

"Sit with your thoughts, you will know what to do. Stay here until you know. I will take care of your business in town."

For the next three days, every morning Paul went to the sweat lodge, poured water on the hot rocks then prayed with Old Man. They would finish with a plunge into the icy cold river. Paul would dash for the house, teeth chattering, beating his cold limbs with his numb hands. Old Man would come at a measured pace, fry up their breakfast, get in his truck and drive to town. He told Paul he was helping distribute the buffalo meat sometimes by horse and sleigh, or as a spotter with the helicopter crew. Some time in the night he would come back, for he was there every morning when Paul awoke.

Every day now, the newscaster began his segment with a story about the ice glazed snows, the buffalo leaving the Park and the rangers shooting them. Animal rights demonstrators were gathering, but the fierce weather kept them inside the roadside cafes.

Despite the fact that the Park Service continued to butcher and package in a processing plant without their help, without their blessing, some of the Traditionalists prayed for forgiveness and asked that the meat be available to their tribes. It reminded Old Man of the sad days when the people were first put on the reservations, not allowed to hunt, relying completely on commodities - rations from a government wagon. Salt pork was as good as it got. It sickened them as they were used to fresh meat. Then, as now, there was not enough to go around. All around Browning, families and friends began to pack together in houses to save on heating fuel and to stretch food. They couldn't afford to heat the homes they left so the pipes froze and burst and the water flooded and ruined the floors, ate at the walls.

On the first morning as Paul watched Old Man pull away, the one-winged magpie who sat on a branch by the cupboard, attempted to fly. He did a nose dive and ended up on the dog's head, who paid him no mind. Picking up the bird, Paul placed it back on the branch and offered a piece of bread. The magpie stared at him, his beady black eyes darting between the bread and the window. Puffing out his feathers, as if to gain altitude, he made another leap and once again hit the floor. Paul picked him up again and taking him over to the window the intrepid aviator threw himself at the light again and again. "The ole 'wing and a prayer' won't cover you, bird. You'll freeze on the ground if a coyote don't get you first." The magpie, his black and verdant green feathers simmering in the light, pecked at the window looking back at Paul as if to say, "Let me go, it's worth it."

That night Paul asked the Old Man if the magpie was always lying on the floor when he came home. Old Man told him that was true and that come spring he would put him outside. "He won't live long, but he will live well," said Old Man.

That night instead of pacing like a trapped varmint, Paul sat cross-legged warmed by the stove and thought about the magpie. Despite the bread and meat and fruit, despite the warm safe branch, magpie would give it all up to be wild, just to be.

Early the next morning, Paul told Old Man he was ready to leave. Now he knew what to do. No more living off road-kill rations, handouts. He would remind the people that they knew how to fend for themselves, to take back what they needed. It is not right to set aside lands from the original people so that the white culture could claim to be protecting the planet. So that they could reassure themselves that wild places still exist while they systematically destroy all that lived within. Whites hold sacred lands in the same manner that they do a city park, a shopping mall, he told Old Man. They keep the buffalo prisoner, like a zoo, not a dwelling for the soul. What did they know of balance, of sustaining resources. How could they speak to the heart of the land.

"Indian people are the natural stewards of the earth, the cultural memory," he told Old Man. "We are a resource of the earth, are we not too an endangered species? To find balance within, our people need to belong, to take back our wild places, the buffalo. I know now it was why I came back." Old Man sat scanning the radio stations and nodding while Paul told him about the magpie's lesson.

Grabbing his jacket and heading out the door, Paul remembered he was a day late for his hearing. Lucy is going to

be real mad about losing her bail, he thought ruefully. "Screw the court system," he yelled back at Old Man, "I am going before the Tribal Leader's Council. Give them a chance to be warriors."

Cranking on his cold starter, he saw Old Man waving a piece of paper at him from the doorway. Paul dashed back to the house, Old Man held out a crudely drawn map saying, "Go to Gabe. Skunk wagon driver, he's worse." Paul felt his gut turn. "Now it is you who must be brave warrior," said Old Man, his eyes on Paul's stunned face. "Go now, quick, hide with Gabe. They will be looking for you both. I go to the Tribal Leaders and speak for you. See what is to be done."

"How do you know this," Paul whispered. "Did you have a vision? Did Napi come?"

“No,” said Old Man. “Heard it on the radio.”

The matter of fact tone stunned Paul who was expecting spiritual revelation. But Napi, the guide, the trickster, had indeed showed up. As he leaned in to pull the door shut, the magpie made a run for it. Old Man nodded his head, smiled and closed the door.

Climbing slowly back into the cold car, his mind searched for that one definitive moment when another choice would have stayed them to the path back to the reservation with a load of buffalo meat. He could think of none. For a moment he sat staring, yet not seeing through the softly falling snow, his breath clouding the windshield until all was white haze. There had been no accidents, no mistakes on their part. The Creator had chosen this, as much as He had sent him the magpie. There was no way back to before.

##

“Why are you standing there holding your boots? Did we interrupt a little something,” leered Red sizing up Feral and Gabe. “Always liked blondes, don’t you, Gabe. This one’s a little long in the tooth for you, maybe just right for more experienced guy like me.”

“You almost interrupted something,” said Feral. “You just about interrupted a bullet in the head for trespassing, but I was afraid I might hit the dog.”

“Whoa,” laughed Jake, “that’s some welcome.”

Kenny sidled in behind Feral. Facing Gabe, Red and Jake between her and the entrance to the cave, Feral waved her rifle and said, "Move back, I'm out of here. You have tonight. I know you got your problems, but when my old dad finds you, he won't just come in here and drink your coffee and eat your cookies, he'll have your butt for breakfast."

Kenny reached over Feral's shoulder and snatched the rifle from her. For a second, her mouth dropped and she just stood there staring at her empty hands. Swinging around she tried to grab the gun back from a grinning, swaying, side-stepping Indian. Gabe watched Feral make several futile grabs for the rifle while Red and Jake laughed before he said, "Red, make your dumb buddy there give the lady her gun."

"Kenny ain't no buddy of mine and I'm thinking maybe he is only half-dumb. Jake, he's your kin, right? You make him give the nice lady her rifle."

"You know he's Cheyenne, not Sioux," retorted Jake.

"Well you two better cozy up. It always did take a Sioux and a Cheyenne together to stay even with a Blackfeet," said Red.

Jake leapt forward and slugged Red square in the jaw knocking him flat. Standing over him, fists poised, Jake suddenly stepped back and lowered his hands. Red lie on the ground rubbing his chin. Everybody including Jake and Red looked surprised. Nobody spoke.

Feral snatched her rifle from Kenny and using the stock end shoved him out of her way. Striding to the cave entrance, she said, "Well, it's been real entertaining meeting you guys, you got problems to figure out and my advice to you is don't overstay your time here, cause as I said, I am the sweet, accommodating one of the family."

Dragging their gear in the cave, they laid out their bedrolls, cooked up a batch of biscuits and finished a meal of buffalo steaks.

Kenny sat cross-legged rolling coffee grounds in toilet paper. "If I don't get me a real smoke real damn quick, I'm just gonna pack it in. Head down the road. Sneak up on some park ranger." The paper burned too quickly leaving him with one drag that made him cough and a handful of chard grounds that stunk.

"A real Indian would know how to find wild tobacco," said Red.

"Oh yea," replied Jake. "I don't see you scrounging out there for some. I bet your last smoke was one you weaseled from Pete."

"Been gonna quit. At four bucks a pack, buying drugs is cheaper." The darkness outside filled the cave. The fire burned lower. Cisco sniffed the ground for pieces of buffalo steak dropped from their meal.

"Kenny," said Red, "you better get out there and find us some wood or your backside will freeze tonight cause you're guarding the door."

"Remember, I ain't got no pack boots," whined Kenny. "Pete's feet way too small."

"You got feet the size of sleds," replied Red. "Them pointy-toed cowboy boots are just right for plowing. Easy enough to follow your tracks back. Get out there."

"Hey Red, why are you such a hard ass," Gabe said, using his bread to sop up the last of the buffalo steak juice left on his plate. "He isn't the only one gonna get cold," he said watching Kenny dump an armful of branches by the fire and stomp out again. "Besides, he apparently doesn't know that green branches won't burn."

"I know that little buddy, but I just like making his life miserable. Makes me just feel warm inside. He's a damn pot head. Ain't even good enough for dog food."

Suddenly the air was pierced with a scream. Running out the entrance of the cave in the deepening shadows they could just make out Kenny thrashing around on the ground trying to pull his cowboy boot off. Steam rose from him. "Hot, burn me. Fell in a hole."

Grabbing Kenny's leg, Gabe jerked the boot off. Hot water poured out.

"Well, now, Red. You must feel real, real good about now, huh Red. I believe Kenny is feeling pretty damn miserable."

Straightening up, Gabe came eyeballs to headlights on his pickup, completely exposed without the branches covering it. "Kenny, you got those branches for the fire off my truck." I should throw you back in the hotpot." Kenny whimpered. Red snorted.

"Well let's haul him inside, see how bad the burns are," said Gabe as he and Jake positioned themselves on either side and hoisted up Kenny. "Not that we can do a diddley thing about it."



Red, digging through his parka, suddenly let out a whoop and held up a found cigarette.

"Anybody got a match?"

Kenny, carried like a bag of flour, managed to make a grab for the cigarette. Red knocked his hand out of the way and clamped it bent, between his lips.

"I'm dying, here man can you give me that last smoke. I'd go peaceful."

"If I thought it was that easy, I'd be lighting it at both ends for you right now," said Red, "but I think you are not going quiet, or soon enough. Before this gig is over you are going to be wishing all that was hurting was some boiled tootsies."

Stepping back through the entrance of the cave, Red said, "We are out here screwing off dragging his sorry hide around when we should be making a plan. The Feds are going to figure out eventually that we are not on the rez. Talk to enough people and they are going to know, Gabe, that you and I are cousins and next thing they will come blasting right in here."

"I think we should be thinking about Billy," said Jake. "Get him out of jail. He's taking it for all of us."

"That is a great idea," Red said. "You leave tonight. Take my truck. I'll throw in some gas money, but ya gotta take Kenny with ya."

Gabe pulling Kenny's socks off, frowned at the blisters blooming across the top of his foot. "At least the skin is still attached to the bone," he grimaced. "You might come out of this in a few days with the foot still on." Kenny looked down and let out a howl.

Moving back to the fire, Gabe stretched out, picked a bone off his plate and gnawing on it said, "I'm thinking we stay quiet for a day or so till we find out how big the trouble is. If the guy is all right, then we all go home. What is the worse they can get on us, especially you guys. All you did was load up a little meat. I'm the one with my butt in a sling. Speaking of that meat, where is the rest of it anyway?" asked Gabe. "Come morning I had planned to go over to where we were butchering and get some, but you're telling me it all ended up at the game station and you took it from there?"

"Ya, a lot of it. It weighed my truck down to the axel," said Red, "so I left most of it there at the ranch. Get it later. Pete will keep some for lending us pack stuff. Got a little some back in the truck. Enough to go a couple more feeds. Hell," he added, "the Park is full of game. This is our happy hunting ground."

"Oh there is going to be some hunting alright, but just who is gonna end up with their hide tacked to the side of the shed remains to be seen. Anybody got a gun, besides me?" asked Gabe.

"We were just here to ride in the rodeo," said Jake. I always keep a rifle in my pickup but it's parked at the Crow's place outa gas."

From over in the corner, Kenny moaned in his sleep.

"Problem is, while I got a gun I don't have much in the

way of ammo. But if I had me an extra bullet, I might just use it to put that one out of his misery," said Red jerking his head toward Kenny. For once, Jake or Gabe did not intercede. 

##

Paul hunkered down on his bed and pulled the covers over his head. He had gone to his house to get supplies after parking his truck in the crowded tribal office lot. If only he could wake up again, feel alive, feel certain like he had this morning at Old Man's. Throwing sleeping bags, boots, clothes and food in a couple of canvas bags, he decided he'd take a moment to enjoy his mattress, feel sorry for himself and to call Lucy.

"I haven't heard anything from Red." Lucy's voice was flat. "He's gone off before but it has been four days since he called me from Bozeman and all he talked about then was a Crow beating him out of the big money at the rodeo."

"Can't they get anything out of that Sioux they picked up at the game station? Red wasn't alone there," Paul said.

"When I came to bail you out, the Sioux was yelling about the Blackfeet being mongrels, leaving him with all the trouble. Other than that, all I know is what I hear on the news. Your name comes up for missing your hearing and they are sure looking hard for Gabriel. Leroy is still in jail. Nobody will make his bail and if the snowmobiler guy dies, it's going to be bad."

"Sorry about the bail, I will pay you back. I'm not sure what I am going to do," said Paul spreading the map Old Man had given him on the kitchen counter. "Old Man says I've got to go to Gabe. That Gabe, he's a wild man. He could get us in more trouble. I am not going to end up in prison on account of some stupid sled head who got himself killed." Paul's words collided. His heart jumped in his chest. "Maybe I will have to turn myself in before this is over, but damn it, I didn't come back to have it end like this. We need a fast horse and a good shield."

"You and Gabe need a smart lawyer with a fast mouth," said Lucy.

CHAPTER 10

# NOW WE GOT BEAR TROUBLE

Stoking the fire, Gabe poured the last of the coffee grounds in the pot. "Gotta make a run to the quick stop for some more coffee. Didn't plan on providing for a full winter camp." The cave, though smelling like rotten eggs from the sulfur pools, was surprisingly warm given the raw January dawn temperature outside.

Jake sat up in his bag. "I been thinking, wondering just why in the hell I came. Billy won't tell them it's me. I could just take a hike back home and sit tight. I don't need to be out here with you bunch. I didn't lasso any sled head."

"Now Jake," said Red, "don't be taking this to mean I'd miss ya. It's just that we don't know how much trouble we got and I don't detect any real loyalty coming from your direction. You punk, you'd turn on us in a bronc buckin minute."

"Gotta say I agree with Red," said Gabe. "Besides, how are you going to get anywhere? My truck's froze up and Red's sitting on his keys. You start hitchhiking and the only ones gonna pick you up are park rangers or state patrol. These snow machine driving idiots leave their rigs in West Yellowstone. That's a lot of miles in 30 degrees below."

Kenny's moans got louder. "Ooh, my feet are hurtin. I need a cigarette bad. Anybody spare a smoke?" Hoisting himself up on one elbow, he stared at them in turn, searching for telltale signs that somebody was holding out on him. "Even one drag?"

Red slowly reached in his jacket and pulled out a can of

tobacco. Shaking it toward Kenny, he said, "Too bad I don't have any papers, you could roll your own."

Kenny scrambled out his bag and attempted to get to his feet. Letting out a yelp, he fell back, his face contorted in pain. "God, my foot hurts somethin' awful." His eyes kept shifting from his feet to the can of tobacco Red kept shaking.

"You must not want a smoke real, real bad," said Red. "You too damn lazy to get your hide out of bed, that's all. Maybe I will find me some papers and roll some of this fine tobacco," he said fishing around his other pockets.

Kenny gingerly pulled off what was left of the sock that Gabe had cut last night after they drug him back in the cave.

"Which reminds me, Kenny, are you all out of that funny grass you been suckin down since I first laid eyes on you?"

Red's voice was mocking. Kenny nodded, his chin slumped to his chest.

Gabe leaned over and picking up Kenny's injured foot, shook his head, muttering, "Too bad, you are gonna need it. You've got more blisters than skin left." Kenny lay back down, his arms covering his eyes.

"Just nothing like that first cup of coffee and smoke," drawled Red sipping from a blue chipped cup and pulling on the butt. The smoke traveled fast like a messenger right to Kenny.

The stiff cold morning creaked in its old bones. Vapor rose off the hot pools, the sun climbed pink and gold to the horizon and stared across at the moon trying to slip away. Gabe added another log to the fire. Staring into the coffee pot, he wondered as he swirled them if the grounds would even color the water brown. He had brought enough for himself for a week. It had been a long night.

Kenny lay with the sleeping bag thrown over him covering everything but his blistered, swollen feet sticking out the bottom. His thin breathing was punctuated by an occasional snort as he dozed.

Jake propped up on one arm watching Gabe waiting for a good reason to get up.

"This is the last of it," said Gabe, slicing the half frozen buffalo steaks into the skillet. The searing meat crackled in the fat." Why didn't you bring more food with you from Pete's?"

"Didn't I tell you? We got a bag of pinto beans and a side

of bacon," said Red. "Guess Pete ran out of generosity after that and figured we could hunt something down."

"Be good if you'd brought some bullets. Pistol whipping a moose to death is not my idea of good hunting," said Gabe snickering.

"Let's use ole Kenny here as bait and get us a bear," said Red. "That way, we'd have meat and a nice rug too." Red climbed out of his bag and standing at the cave entrance proceeded to pee an arch into one of the pools.

"Take it way outside, man. I don't want any piss marking the entrance," yelled Gabe.

"Hey, I'm thinking ahead, I hide my tracks, I peed in the pool."

"Real glad you did that, seeing as how these pools are all connected and the stream flows this way. Probably end up drinking it." Gabe growled.

"Quick, hand me your rifle, man," whispered Red shoving his part back in his pants. "Breakfast is headed this way."

Gabe tossed the gun to Red just as a bull elk and two of his harem sauntered by the cave entrance. Catching their scent, the elk turned and plunged through the snow leaping over the hot pools with grace.

Red lowered the rifle cussing, "No damn butt shot." Just then one of the cows turned to look back. Red nailed her right in the head. She went down with a thud and in a moment, the bull and cow disappeared into the trees.

"Good shot. Practically in the frying pan," said Red.

“Come on, we gotta get to skinin’, ole Red is hungry.” 

Gabe nodded as he scanned the horizon. Sizing up the job, Gabe knew skinning and cutting up the elk was going to be a big job. He had the only skinning knife and no saw for cutting the bones. Red hacked away with a pocket knife.

The air was cold and a grey mist settled depositing ice droplets on the tips of tree branches and bushes and mixed with their sweat.

“Some hunters,” sneered Jake. “Two guns only one with bullets, one knife between ya.”

“Okay, prick,” said Red, “I got a couple of bullets. One for you. What have you done to provide lately.”

“I’m here holding the rifle, I’m standing between you and somethin’ getting at you,” Jake said gesturing toward the dark line of trees lining the horizon.

“I sure don’t like living next door to a gut pile,” said Gabe as he pulled the intestines loose from the belly cavity. “Like a special invite for bears and other man-eating critters.”

“You scared of a little bear,” joked Red. “They are all sleepin’. Denned up, passed out.”

“One of those big bastards blasts through that cave door we’ll see who is scared,” replied Gabe. Yellowstone has one bear for every 40 miles, about 500 living in Yellowstone eco-system. They need that much room just to get along with each other. We showed up uninvited.”

Jake spun around and raised the rifle. After a minute he lowered it and forced a grin. “Just making sure they are hibernating," he said with edge.

"Course they are, but they get restless, especially if they went to den skinny. They smell this blood and guts and they will come alive real quick. Finish off with a side of Indian," Gabe chortled.

Dressing out the elk, skinning and cutting up the meat in hunks took the two men most of the day. Jake had never butchered before and wasn't inclined to learn. Kenny lay in the cave alternating between snores, moans and yells for water and cigarettes.

By dusk, all the butchering they could do was done. "It's a good 100 feet from the cave," said Red. "No problem with bears. They'll just sit out here and suck up guts like noodles."

Washing the blood off their bodies, they threw their clothes in a hot pool to soak.

"Better to smell like rotten eggs than a ripe kill," said Gabe. "I'd burn em, but I only planned on a week here so I don't have much to wear."

With four men in the confined area, the cave heated up like a sauna. Sitting around the fire in their shorts, they tried out the tender elk steak.

"Jesus, just when I thought it couldn't stink any worse in here, what is that?" yelled Jake.  All eyes turned to Kenny.

Standing over him, Red reached down and jerked back the sleeping bag. Kenny moaned and rolled over, a brown puddle oozed, spreading across the ground as fresh stink assailed their nostrils.

“He’s shit all over himself,” yelled Red. “What is wrong with him!” I say we drag him out and dump him on that ripe gut pile. Oh man, how can you touch him,” said Red recoiling as Gabe felt Kenny’s flushed face.

“He is not just sleeping,” stated Gabe, “he is sick, burning up. We need to get him back to town.”

Jake stepped forward. “Red, you lend me your pickup and I will take him in. Leave him at that ranger station we saw on the way here. I will drive your pickup to Pete’s where I got my rig.”

Red’s eyes traveled from Gabe to Jake, Kenny and back again.

“Can’t lend him mine,” said Gabe. “It won’t make it. Outa gas, oil pan leaking.”

“This pile of crap,” said Red jerking his head toward Kenny, “isn’t worth losing my pickup over.”

“Red, come on.” Gabe gave Red a shove. “You been wanting to get rid of this guy, now here is your chance.”

“I swear to you that I will leave your rig at Pete’s,” implored Jake.

“Get out of here and take that pile of dung with you.” Red tossed the keys at Jake.

Wrapping Kenny like a mummy, Jake and Gabe carried him down the path to where Red had parked the pickup. “He’s gotta go back here,” said Jake. The camper cover over the truck bed would not be warm, but would break the wind. “He is too sick to sit up and I don’t want him lying all over me so

I can't drive."

"Better drive fast, he won't last long if he gets hypothermia too," said Gabe, slamming the tailgate and watching the pickup belch blue smoke and pull slowly out of the clearing.

Taking the long way around, Gabe breathed deep and paused to lean against a tree. Need to clear my head of the stink of that cave and this whole mess, he thought. Think through a plan. How is it that one day I am Tribal Fish and Game and the next a fugitive. I've done nothing wrong. Only right things. The herd would have burst their lungs and bled to death if we had not stopped the snow machines.

Pushing through the tall dead grass, out of the corner of one eye he caught a glimpse of a brown shaggy head poking its big black nose up sniffing the air. The nostril holes looked like the barrel end of a shotgun.

Standing completely still, hardly breathing, Gabe cursed himself for not having a gun. Careless, foolish. He knew better than to be out here without one. Slowly the bear stood up its head bobbing from side to side. His rancid breath traveled the short distance between them. Stomach churning though it was, it meant the wind was blowing the bear's scent to Gabe not the other way around. Bears can't see well and Gabe hoped he looked like a tree, albeit not a very big one. The bear's yellow claws hanging down over his belly were the length of Gabe's hands.

Seconds passed like hours. Slowly turning his head, Gabe could just make out the cave. Red was standing in the entrance smoking a cigarette. Cisco was at his side. Gabe prayed Red would not call to him or that the dog wouldn't spot him. Suddenly the bear's head swung around towards Red. Dropping on all fours he shuffled back, then leaned forward trying to make out what was bold enough to be setting up housekeeping in his territory. Abruptly he turned and headed back into the brush. Gabe ran the hundred-yard dash in record time.

Pushing past the startled Red, Gabe grabbed his rifle and filled the magazine with shells.

"What the hell!" said Red.

"Big hump back, grizzly, ten feet tall, I swear," yelled Gabe. "He saw you. He'll be back."

"Hell yes, this is all we need. I told you, a rug for our new home," said Red.

"Pretty dangerous way to furnish the living room," Gabe said. "He'll start by bothering the gut pile and come looking for more choice cuts."

"Maybe he's so big he won't fit through the cave door."

"Well, I ain't counting on that," said Gabe snapping the rifle bolt. "Muzzle the dog and tie him up."

Peering out the cave entrance, Gabe saw the bear peering at them from a stand of poplars. The gut pile aroma and the dining magpies hopping and chattering on the kill site issued a special invitation.

"Maybe we can scare him away," said Red reaching for his rifle.

“Scare a grizzly off a feeding,” spit Gabe holding tight to the gun. “You’ll just remind him we’re dessert. I knew killing that elk this close was a mistake.”

“Sure, easy to say now,” said Red. “Now that you just ate your fill. How did you expect us to drag 500 pounds of dead weight somewhere more to your liking? How, big shot game expert.”

The bear slowly ambled toward the bone pile making a wide circle around the mouth of the cave all the while squinting his small pig eyes, trying to figure them out. Stopping to sniff the air, he grabbed a mouthful and begin to eat. The only sound was the crunch of the dead elk’s backbone.

“What the hell are we gonna do now,” moaned Red. “We can’t stand here day and night until he comes looking for us. We got all this meat hanging in the trees. And we can’t make it in your pickup cause if it won’t start right away he’ll just rip the doors off it like a tuna can.”

“I thought you said you weren’t scared of bears.” Gabe settled down with the rifle across his knees. “Get you own gun. It will take both of us to stop him if he starts coming.”

“Maybe we better find a tree to climb,” said Red.

“Ordinarily I would agree,” said Gabe, “but the only ones tall enough around here are behind the bear.”

“Damnit.”

“Ditto,” replied Gabe.

All afternoon Gabe and Red kept watch rotating inside the cave to warm up while the bear ate and slept. Toward evening,

Red began to relax. "I don't think he cares about us. He knows we belong out here same as him."

Gabe grinned, "It just ain't our time yet. Ordinarily, bears sleep during the day and maraud at night," replied Gabe. "My guess is he is saving us for later. For dessert."

Red nervously sighted his scope on the head of the bear.

As the twilight settled and waning light tinted the vapor clouds and snow mounds pink and yellow, the landscape took on a cake-icing look. Gabe and Red peering out into the deepening shadows couldn't imagine how anything horrible including this "Ursus horribilis" stalking them could happen in this surreal setting. With the bear sleeping again, all seemed natural, pastoral.

Cisco muzzled so he couldn't bark, growled deep in his throat. From out of the clearing, another bear with two cubs ambled toward the bone pile. The sleeping diner reared up and let out a roar. The cubs squealed and ran back into the trees. Mama bear stood her ground and moved slowly but menacingly forward, the hair along her back standing straight up silhouetting the huge grizzly hump. Round and round the carcass they stepped in the face off. Mama Bear with two cubs to feed most determined it was now her turn.

"I hope they don't duke it out," said Gabe. "A dead bear added to the elk's gut pile would draw crowds of their relatives for hundreds of miles. They eat each other too, you know. That male will eat those cubs if Big Mama loses. And the stench will make this rotten egg sulfur pool smell like sweet grass."

"This lesson in nature watching is fuckin fine," whispered Red, "but we lose no matter which one of them wins. What is your plan?"

"I'm still thinking."

"Fire our rifles, that will scare them off," yelled Red.

"Only if they start coming this way. We need to conserve ammo."

The bears continued their slow cross over walk around the bone pile with every once in a while taking a swipe at each other.

Gabe whispered, "If those claws connect expect an arm hanging by a tendon or your head ripped off. I heard a bear ate a hiker right down to his boots up on Chief Mountain last

summer. Left the knapsack with a peanut butter sandwich still in it."

"Whoa, I thought they'd go for peanut butter. It's one of my favorites," Red said. "Beats the hell out of chewing hiking boots."

Two hours went by. The bears would make a false charge and about half way through sit down and stare at each other. Occasionally one or the other would doze.

"I can't just sit here all night," whined Red. As if on cue, Cisco burst through the cave opening and howling like a banshee made straight for the bears.

"What the hell," yelled Gabe, "how'd he get loose! Grab those sticks out of the fire bears don't like flames."

Within about 50 feet, Cisco had sized up his prey and

decided maybe not. Maybe later. Maybe run like the wind back to where he came from with both bears closing in fast.

Gabe shot his rifle in the air over their heads. Red threw flaming sticks as fast as he could grab them from the fire.

About 20 feet from where the two men stood the bears stopped short. Cisco certain he had stopped them felt his confidence soar. He started barking so hard and loud that his body lifted off the ground each time as though he had springs for feet. Red grabbed a frying pan and beat it with the lid, all the while whooping and hollering. The clamor coupled with the gun shots and an occasional flame missile finally got the best of the bruins. They turned and high-tailed back into the bush without even stopping at the gut pile for a nibble.

Weak with relief, the two men collapsed on the ground in a heap laughing. Cisco ran in circles licking their faces.

Hungry and tired they headed into the cave. “Maybe we better move tomorrow. The neighborhood has just gone to hell,” quipped Gabe. Stoking the fire, Gabe stared into the flames. “Seriously now we need to find another spot. Those bears will be back, maybe even tonight,” he said grimly.

Red rummaged through his gear and finally located his whiskey bottle. Tilting it toward Gabe who shook his head no, Red tipped it back for a good long swallow. “If I am going to get et, ole Red wants to be drunk.”

“Hootch will just make you crazy and then I end up fighting you and the bears. Put it away Red, this is no regular brawl. Them fight to kill and eat.”

Red looked at the bottle, then at Gabe. Lifting it to his lips he took a short swig, then stuck it back in his bag. “Party’s over I guess. We gonna want to sleep here tonight?” said Red. They were eating the last of the cold biscuits. No fire, no cooking tonight.

“Looking for a new cave at night may not be a great idea and its too damn cold to sleep outside, but I am spooked too,” replied Gabe.

Suddenly Cisco was on his feet a with deep growl the fur rising along his back.

“Oh shit, already! Grab your fire sticks, I got the rifle.”

Looking over at Cisco, Gabe could see the dog relax, watchful, but not bristling. Then Gabe heard the sound of

snow crunching, a whistle and Jake burst through the entrance.

“Don’t shoot me man, it’s me, Jake. Did you know there’s a hump back bear sitting out there about a hundred yards away just watching? I was figuring I would be up a tree before I made this cave.”

Again Cisco bristled and made a leap for the door. Spinning around Gabe grabbed him by the collar and tied his leash around a rock. Leaning out the entrance, rifle in hand, he could just barely see a dark mound moving slow against the tree line. Only one, wonder where Mama went.

“There is only one way in and out of here and this cave is too small for us and a grizzly. Think. Where’s some place high where he can’t reach,” Gabe’s cheek muscles twitched.

Red dove for his bottle. Gabe slapped it out of his hand

and it smashed against the rocks. "I need you man, all of you." 

"What about that ledge the truck is sitting under. Those rocks are at least 10 feet high, he can't be taller than that. We can climb on the pickup and boost ourselves up," said Jake. "I was eying it in case I couldn't make the cave before the bear did."

"The bear can climb on the pickup too," said Red.

"We just won't let him get that close," said Gabe. "Grab those clothes and some branches, I got a little gasoline in a can in the pickup. Bears hate fire," he said reassuringly.

Wearily they pulled on their jackets, gloves and pack boots. Jake grabbed sleeping bags while Red took clothes and a few long sticks from their wood pile. Slipping out the opening a full moon in a cloudless night sky guided their steps. They couldn't see the bear. They hoped he couldn't smell them. But they knew different.

"What's ya gonna do with this noisy dog," said Jake as they hurried toward the truck.

"Muzzle him and put him in the pickup. He'll crawl under the seat if he's scared enough," said Gabe. "And by the way, what the hell are you doing back here and what did you do with Kenny?"

"Where's my rig?" pressed Red.

Before he could answer, they heard a "woof" and a rustle in the nearby brush.

"Climb quick," ordered Gabe as he shoved Cisco through the door of the pickup. Above him he could hear Red grunting as he struggled up the sheer cliff.

"Get over and let me up," hollered Jake as the rustling grew louder. Scrambling up the rock wall like a goat, he hauled his body over the top and leaning down he grabbed Red by the back of his jacket and pulled. Huffing like a locomotive, Red cussed and scraped his way up the rough face. "Shove your feet in those holes like they was steps, you idiot. Blackfeet – more like slow feet," muttered Jake. Below him he could hear Red cussing all Sioux, questioning their parentage.

"Save your fight for the bear. Haul ass!"

Gabe stood on the cab of the pickup and prayed Red would hurry. The bear was somewhere on the ground close to the pickup. Close enough for Gabe to hear his teeth clicky, clicky,

clicky. Inside the pickup Cisco raced from side to side, froth forming around the muzzle forcing his jaws together.

Looking down, Gabe could see the griz moving around the pickup. If he stands up, his head will be about where my crotch is he thought. Again, that stench of bear breath like a plume of everything rotten in the world drifted across his face. And once again, Gabe knew they just might be lucky, cause the wind was blowing their scent away from the bear. Bears are really near-sighted and their hearing isn't nearly as keen as their sense of smell.

Gabe felt the truck begin to rock as the bear stood up and bumped against it. Trying to keep his balance and standing very still he could see the bear's head rise like some macabre monster from under a bed as he sniffed the air and stared at the cliff where Red hung almost to the top. 

Gabe could dimly see that if Red didn't fall, if he could make one more step, then the top, he would be out of reach. He is making a damn racket thought Gabe. Bears may not hear well, but they aren't deaf.

The bear cocked his head like he was trying to figure out this whole deal. Dropping on all fours, he waddled around the other side of the truck and rubbed against it. Inside, Cisco finally lay quiet, his paws covering his eyes.

With a mighty heave, Jake pulled Red over the top. Loose rocks clattered down startling the bear who reared up, ran around the truck, peered up the rock ledge. Jake and Red lay very still. Still on its hind legs, griz looked around until his beady eyes fastened on Gabe. Gabe stopped breathing. The griz dropped down took a few steps back and started to paw at the ground.

Jake yelled, "Grab it," as he dropped a heavy branch over the face of the cliff. Leaping from the roof of the truck cab, Gabe lunged for the branch and scrambled up the rocks. Behind him he could hear the grizzly's teeth clicking and rocks and dirt flying as the bruin worked up a charge.

Midway Gabe pumped his foot frantically in the air. He couldn't find a hold or make himself look down. Flailing, his leg scouring the rough face, he finally connected with rock. With Red pulling on one side and Jake on the other, Gabe flopped over the top, stretched out on his stomach. All the air gone out of him. Their breath came in ragged gasps as if they had held it forever.

"Got a match?" said Red frantically feeling through his pockets. "I gotta light these," he said holding up a stick with gas soaked rags, his hands shaking. Down below the bear continued to roar and fling rocks and dirt building up a head of steam.

"Just shoot the son a bitch," yelled Jake.

"No," said Gabe. "He's just being a bear and pretty soon he's gonna get bored and go home. We kill him, we'll find out what bear trouble is all about."

"Hey man, you act like you are defending your home. We can find another cave. We can plumb get the hell out of here. Why are we staying here anyway?" Jake's voice went up several notches.

Down below the bruin paced back and forth churning up mud and snow and pawing the ground like a bull. A low growl and the click-click of the teeth raised their fear level a degree a second. Suddenly the bear stopped, cocked his head, spun around and ran toward the side of the bank where the slope was more gradual.

"Shit, he knows the way around, he'll come get us from behind," yelled Red. "Get him to change his mind, man, he's gonna get us."

"Light these rags, I am going to drop them on him." said Gabe.

"Just shoot the son a bitch," yelled Jake. "What are you waiting for?"

Gabe leaned over as far as the bank would hold him and whistled. The bear stopped digging his way up the cliff and cocked his head in their direction. Gabe whistled again. The bear side-stepped his way to where he was just below them. Tilting his head one way and then the other sniffing the air, the bear tried to figure out where the sound was coming from. He knew it was somewhere on top of the cliff, but his senses relied on smell and the wind was still shifted away from him. Perched ten feet above the bear, Gabe felt like he could touch him. He could sure smell him.



He dropped the burning rag. It landed on the bear's head, then fell at his feet. The stink of burning hair added to the aroma of bear breath, greasy wet hide and their own fear and sweat. The bear jumped back. Then with a roar he grabbed the burning stick in his teeth. Letting out a bellow, his red tongue lolling, he looked around for someone to punish for his pain.

Then the bear remembered. He had these three idiots waiting for him just over head. Whirling around, ears pinned back, hair along his hump ridge standing on end, he charged like a locomotive sideways up the cliff. Rocks the size of bowling balls rolled out from under his frantically churning feet. Sliding one foot for every two gained, the bear grunted and pushed his way toward them.

"They are supposed to run from fire," murmured Gabe, "not eat it."

"They are supposed to like eating peanut butter better than eating hiking boots too," Red yelled.

"Just shoot the son-a-bitch," yelled Jake.

"Okay, already, I will," yelled Gabe, bracing his rifle and firing. The blast of the 300 Magnum knocked him back.

The awful thrashing noise stopped. Gabe crawled back to the edge and started to lean over the ledge. As he did, the bear stood up – all eight feet of him – his chin resting on the ledge, eye balling Gabe, his huge black nostrils looking like the business end of a shotgun. Gabe froze. The gates of hell were open, the stink bellowing out made his stomach roll as the teeth began that terrible clacking sound. Red and Gabe both fired. For a second the bear just stood there, resting his chin on the ledge, the hate fever dimming in his eyes. Then with a crash he tumbled down the incline landing in the back of the pickup.

"Shit, he just won't go away, now will he," said Red.

"We just thought we had bear trouble, now we got bear trouble," said Gabe.

## CHAPTER 11

# ONE IN THE BED, ONE IN THE BUSH

"Lucy," Paul, huddled in a phone booth, spoke low. "I am going to go by Gabe's place, check it out. Maybe he's there, maybe Old Man is wrong. But if he's not, he's freezing his ass off in Yellowstone. I have got to go to him. We are both in this."

"Paul, should you do this thing? Gabe's my cousin and I'm scared for him, but you should stay here, talk to the tribal attorney. Don't make it worse for all of you. Gabe knows how to take care of himself in the mountains. You are soft from Seattle, but you know how to talk your way around the system."

"Old Man says go. He will speak to the tribal leader's

council. They will get the lawyers if that is what is needed." The line went dead. Pushing open the frost covered door, he pulled his coat collar high, keeping his head down and made for his pickup. Brushing the snow off the windshield, he heard a gruff voice behind him over an engine idle.

"I ain't seen ya," said the Browning patrolman. "I don't want to have to see ya again for a while." Gunning the big engine, the officer sped out of the parking lot.

Lonesome whinnies greeted him as he pulled into Gabe's place. No lights, no smoke from the chimney. The house was empty and cold. Filling the water tank and throwing down some hay, he decided to turn the horses out to pasture. Better to have them running loose looking for grass than corralled

starving, he thought. It might be awhile before we get back to them. Shifting low, he circled the house, the barn and reluctantly headed down the highway.

##

Red's whole body shook, tears ran down his face as he doubled over laughing.

"What the hell is so funny," said Gabe. "We got some major shit goin down here and you are laughing your ass off."

Jake stood looking at the beast lying flat on his back in pickup bed. "You finally shot the son-a-bitch."

"Alright, listen up," commanded Gabe. "We may be the red guys, but we have killed a grizzly which is a protected species in a national park where hunting is against federal law. And he is stretched out in my pickup. And, just in case you forget, we are supposed to lie low. Keep still, quiet, out of trouble. Hiding."

Jake, cocked his head in the direction of the bear and said. "Guess this ain't cool."

Red slumped to the ground, weak from laughter and relief.

"When the other bears get wind of this they will come eat this guy and tear my truck to shit. Probably not before the rangers get here and find him plugged full of lead in the head though," moaned Gabe. "How are we gonna move him. He's gotta weigh close to 700 pounds give or take a hundred."

"Back this hummer around and head it up the embankment, he'll fall out, least ways we can drag him out," offered Red.

"If it will start," countered Gabe. Jerking open the door, he stepped back as Cisco shot through the door, his muzzle still clamped shut with the strap.

Grinding down the last of the battery, Gabe looked over at his bleary companions. "Let's get some sleep. Let this guy alert the other bears tonight. But, Jake, you take the first watch. By the way, where is Kenny?"

"Where's my pickup," Red demanded.

"You ought to be glad to see me, I could have ended up like Billy," Jake said. "Made it to West Yellowstone and there were cops and park ranger dudes everywhere. I parked the rig downtown, hoofed it out to the truck stop and be dammed, if there wasn't state patrol out there. Pistol-totin badge carrying lawmen all over the place. Since the only semi headed anywhere was going this direction, I took it."

"You dumb fuck. You left my pickup parked with that scum Kenny rottin' in the back?"

"Pretty much," Jake said.

Gabe shook his head in disbelief. "Kenny can't make it left outside like that. We'll end up with another dead one on our list to be blamed for."

"You left my pickup?" Red's outrage was escalating.

"Kenny is gonna die," said Gabe.

"Nah, I told the trucker to call the hospital to go and get him. I told him it wasn't our fault Kenny fell in a pot. Serves him right for smoking pot. Pot head fell in a hotpot. That's kind of funny, don't ya think." Jake's voice trailed off as he looked over at the fuming Red.

Red said, "I'm gonna stew you in a hotpot if I lose my rig over this."

"That will be the least of our trouble," countered Gabe.

Gabe nodded to Jake, "See if you can stay awake for a while. One of them bears decide to come through that hole, shoot, but only if he is breathing down your neck. We are gonna end up with a regular bone yard out here."

"Hey, we gotta find a new camp in the morning I'm thinking," said Red. Reaching inside his jacket he pulled out a package of cigarettes and lit one. Seeing Jake and Gabe stare at him with contempt, he added, "Hey, I was trying to spare Kenny's health, smoking ain't good for ya."

Light slowly filled the entrance of the cave. The exhausted men slept deeply. Cisco raised his head and whimpered. Going to Gabe, he licked his face. Gabe moaned and pushed the dog away. "I like you dawg, but your breath smells like the back end of a badger." Cisco ran to the door and back to Gabe whimpering.

"Don't you think the charm has worn off this place what with rotting carcasses everywhere," said Feral as she pushed past the snoring Red whose turn it was to serve as lookout. "Couldn't you just plug a squirrel like any other hungry tourist, did you have to kill an elk at the front door and a griz in the backyard?"

"Morning, Feral. I take it you are here to collect the rent," said Gabe climbing out of his sleeping bag. "Glad to see you are your usual mouthy self."

"Rent, my ass. I served you an eviction notice the day you moved in."

"I'll rent your pretty ass alright," said Red propping himself up in the door way.

Kicking at Red, she leaned in toward Gabe. "You boys don't get it. A hideout is just that. You hide. Lay low. You don't shoot federally protected game. You don't shoot anything in a national park. And at the very top of that list of what not to shoot is a grizzly."

"I know," said Gabe. "He tried to eat us. Besides, we – us Indians – have the right to hunt in parks, comes with the treaty."

"How lame can you be? What stupid stunt have you got in mind next?" Feral said.

Off in the distance Red could hear someone yelling, more like howling. It sounded like a coyote from Chicago. Not quite legitimate. He waved at them to be quiet.

"Oooh," the sound echoed in the quiet morning.

"That sounds like one sick puppy or my buddy Paul," said Gabe. Stepping to the door of the cave, he let go of a howl followed by a few yelps.

"There goes the neighborhood," said Red with a rude gesture in the direction of Paul.

"Oh shit, this is so pathetic," said Feral. "Indians playing at being Indian."

Paul trudged up the path, a heavy gunny sack slung over his shoulder. Stopping at the pickup he let out a yell. "Did you know you got a hitchhiker?"

"Yup. What took you so long, man," said Gabe.

"Hmm, a couple nights in jail, a couple of nights with Old Man and Old Man's magpie, now a manslaughter charge, a few things like that," replied Paul.

"He didn't make it?" asked Gabe.

"Well, he is not far from it. Seems when a guy runs his snow machine over his buddy's leg and he starts to bleed, it's all downhill. Make some coffee, man I need it," Paul said tossing Gabe a bag.

"Dammit all to hell and back that sucker might die," yelled Red. Then scratching his head, he said "Now wait a sec. I got my head screwed around. I got nothing to do with running over the asshole. I just went on an honor ride to liberate the meat. It's you boys that got the real trouble. I could dance out of here. And you showing up, hell, makes it that much easier to leave."

Paul gave him a long look, shrugged and squatted down by the fire.

"Who is stopping you, man," said Jake.

"For starters, dumb ass, you lost my truck," said Red.

"That is why I came this morning," said Feral. "It is all over the news. They are focused on Browning right now. But it is just a matter of time before they link this nitwit," she said pointing at Red, "and the meat caper with the hurt snowmobiler. Plus the fact that you all know each other really well. I'd say you can't afford the rent on this place any longer. With the dead animal littering you've done, you will be arrested for that as well."

For a moment the only sound was the crackling of the fire.

"Paul, you got a vehicle that runs," said Gabe.

"Yea, but where to?"

## CHAPTER 12

# BIG BIRD

Lucy sat drinking her coffee across from Old Man. She stared into the mug swirling the brew hoping the answers would float to the surface. And waited. Old Man spooned three tablespoons of sugar into the cup. He added a dollop of canned milk and took a test sip, added more sugar. Smacking his lips, he nodded, "Good."

The heat from the wood stove made her sweat. She had asked Old Man where Gabe and now, Paul were. He had not answered. She knew he had heard.

Getting up from her chair she went to the window and stared out at the white expanse. The snow was half way up the window. It had been snowing since yesterday and the wind had created huge drifts. Some were over her head, but in other places, the ground was blown bare exposing dirty patches of yellow grass. Old Man had shoveled a tunnel from the front door to the barn and to the shed where he parked his pickup. She had walked the last quarter-mile from the road to the house concerned that the highway department didn't plow this far in. She had no idea how he got out, but he always did.

"Red come home yet?" asked Old Man.

"No," she replied. "Never gone this long with no call. I'm beginning to wonder if he is with Gabe."

"Gabe, Red and Paul hung together as little ones," said Old Man. "Paul's grandfather, Heavy Shield, used to take the boys into Glacier and Yellowstone, the only land besides the reservation that didn't belong to white ranchers – only to the Feds."

"Red and Paul hate each other now," she whispered.

"Yes," he said his eyes boring into her. "It is over a woman. When a man turns his back on his relatives, his friends, it is usually a woman."

She waited staring into her cup. "I didn't think he was ever coming back."

Old Man got up and putting on his jacket, called to the dog. "Feed the horses," he said.

Lucy watched him trudge to the barn, his frame bent like an old pine tree swaying against the wind. Shrugging, she pulled on her coat and begin the cold walk back to her car.

##

Paul had brought sweet rolls, sticky, with strawberry jam and white, chalky icing. They ate the whole package. Feral kept prodding them with questions about where and when they were headed out.

At first the noise sounded like a snow machine but the closer it got, they knew it was a helicopter. It flew low and hovered over the pickup, the nose and cab exposed from Kenny pulling the branches off it to use for firewood. The bear in the back, legs spread wide, was hard to miss. Next the copter flew over the dead elk which was now just a bone pile. Feral could see her horse snorting and kicking up snow.

"You rode in," said Gabe.

"Yea, how else do you think I could sneak up on you. I just follow the buffalo, they follow the snow machine trails and I stay where the snow isn't too deep. That's not hard to do with

the pitiful snowfall and wind this year. My horse is a big draft. Feet the size of washtubs."

"Forget the damn horse and the punta who rode in on it," said Red. "There is a copter overhead looking down our shorts."

"I don't think it can land close," said Gabe. "There's no place where there aren't trees, even if they are small ones. That is why I like it here. It's hard to get at."

"Yea, if that is true," said Feral, "why is it every time I come here seems like a new bus load of visitors shows up. And don't forget I caught you buck naked the first time and you never heard me coming."

Gabe slid through the cave door, staying close to the sides and looked out. The copter hovered. Gabe could see the guy sitting beside the pilot lean out and scan the site through a pair of field glasses. From the air it might not look like a pickup he prayed. Just a little bit of the hood and the nose poking out. The back where the bear lay was still covered in brush and pine-bows.

Another minute and the copter pulled up and began a slow and what everyone hoped would be, a final circle passing overhead. But just as it started to pull away, Feral's horse broke his reins and shot out in the open like a lumbering elephant. Clumps of snow and rocks flew from his huge hooves as he plowed across the meadow. The smell of bear and the noise of the flying machine were too much. He was headed home.

"Good one lady," swore Red.

"You could have shot the copter down," said Jake.

"Why not the horse and the bitch who rode in on him," snorted Red.

Paul and Gabe looked at each other and let out a collective sigh.

"Oh shit, it's go time," said Gabe.

"Well, boys, in addition to those rangers, you can add my old man to the search party," said Feral. "That horse will be back in the barn without me in about an hour."

It's only ten o'clock. It don't get dark till four," said Gabe. "That gives them six hours to find us and less for us to move our ass in some direction. Any good ideas here, guys."

Standing in the dim light of the cave, they looked from one to the other and away again.

Jake said, "Can I borrow your rig, Paul?"

"Don't you think they will be looking for Indians in pickups with Browning license plates?" said Paul.

"I think you ought to give it to him. He's real good with pickups," Red said with a snarl.

"I didn't kill no man, no bears," said Jake.

"Then you better stop hanging around with us who do it on regular basis," Gabe quipped. "And that goes for you too Red. Never thought I'd be worrying about trashing your reputation," he added. "Where can we run and for how long," said Gabe.

Ignoring Red's hard glare, "I had a dream," Paul said quietly. Squatting by the fire, he tossed pine needles in to the blaze. Tiny sparks flared up and quickly died. Jake kept pacing between the door and the fire.

"With all due respect man, not now. Now is the time to haul ass. No time for Indian dreams and visions," Feral said. "No time for ceremonies."

The men watched Paul from under hooded eyes and waited for him to speak. Feral started to say something more when she felt Gabe's hand squeeze her arm.

Paul kept feeding the fire pine needles and watching the flares. "The white man has always taken the best land for himself and pushed us where only the gopher can survive long enough for the snake to eat him. They are killing our buffalo just like the old days."

The men waited nodding their heads. Feral fidgeted.

"What do the white men prize more than the trees, the animals, more than the water and even the air?" he asked. "They hold sacred their buildings. They clear cut a valley and build a house that wears the scars of the ax but gets no break from the wind or shade from the hot sun. The trees that shape it lose their sap and fall to ruin. Those same trees left standing might provide shelter for a thousand years." He continued to add cones and needles to the fire, the sparks snapped in the dim light. The sweet fragrance filled the air. "I say we negotiate with currency they understand. We go to their lodges and hold them ransom until the government gives us our buffalo. We will take them back to our reservations. If they won't hear us, we burn the Park buildings one by one. Fire can also heal." Paul stood up and crossed his arms. Gabe, Red and Jake studied each other with a side-line look. Though no more words were spoken, the men stood up and begin to gather their belongings.

Feral looked from one to the other. "This is it? This is the great plan. You are going to burn down Old Faithful Inn and somehow that will make people listen to you. Let me tell you, Old Faithful is sacred in white man's dreams. You screw with Old Faithful Inn and you will have everybody from school kids to little old ladies carrying baseball bats after your hides."

Kicking out the fire, Gabe looked over at Feral, "You leaving or staying?"

"Hell no, I'm headed home." Feral gripped her rifle. "You are making a major mistake. No American icon is so sacred. Even in the movies, the Indians never burned Old Faithful. You will invoke rage not sympathy and understanding," she said her voice growing quiet. "Don't do this," she said reaching for Gabe's arm. He pulled away without a look.

"Sympathy, understanding, did you just crawl out from under a rock woman," bellowed Red angrily stuffing his clothes in a duffle bag. "Rottin' side pork, bad beans and left over land are the only things handed out to us Indians." The men hurriedly gathered up their gear and loaded elk meat in a couple of canvas bags.

"This is where the trail forks," said Gabe as they stood outside the entrance to the cave.

"You know you can't actually drive there, don't you," said Feral. "The road is closed. The Lodge is closed. It was never winterized like Snow Peak over on the west end."

"We drive as far as we can, then walk," said Gabe.

"Feral," said Red quietly siding up to her, "how about you borrow Paul's truck and give ole Red a lift back to town." I will lay down on the floor and all the cops will see is this beautiful blonde drivin down the road," said Red with a wink.

"Why don't you ask Paul to loan you the pickup," replied Feral loudly.

"You are used to taking, including my woman. I wouldn't lend you shit," said Paul. "But to get rid of you, I might consider it."

"I could use a lift too," said Jake hopefully.

"Well, let's head out, drive as far in as we can, then maybe you get the truck," said Paul.

"That will still leave us 15 miles or more on foot is my guess," said Gabe.

"You will be needing a driver who can talk to the cops, so I will go part way and, I have no horse," said Feral. "But surely you can come up with a better plan?" 

"You and your frigin plans," said Red taking a step toward her, "just shut your face woman."

Gabe jumped to his feet between Red and Feral his eyes boring into Red's, noses almost touching. Red started to lift his hand, then dropped it and stepped back. Gabe turned to look at Feral. She stood very close, very still. After a long moment, she reached up and stroked his cheek. He didn't move. No one spoke. The men looked away from the intimacy. Cisco cocked his head in confusion and begin to jump up on Gabe's leg. Gabe brushed him away without taking his eyes off Feral. The two seemed locked in place.

Finally, Jake said, "Can we take it down the road?"

Dragging their gear and the elk meat out of the cave entrance, they could again hear the copter as it sat down in the direction of the road.

"You don't think those two guys would brave it alone to come down here do you," said Paul.

"No," replied Gabe, "but maybe they found your truck. Where did you park?"

"Hmm, said Paul thumbing toward the highway, "in the general direction where that big bird is now perched."

"The highway is a perfect landing strip," added Feral. "Doesn't anybody in this whole damn crew know how to hide anything!"

"Dammit," exclaimed Red ignoring her, "we have bad luck

 when it comes to trucks."

"Sit tight, they can't take it with them," said Gabe. "Give them some time to look it over, we grab it and go before the law shows up. You all stay here I am going to take a look see."

Feral started to move toward him. "I can tell them it's mine, belongs to one of my ranch hands," she said brushing past him and starting down the trail.

"No. You stay here for now," said Gabe, "we may need you later. They don't need to know we are here," said Gabe grabbing her arm. For a moment she looked like she was going to break free, then shrugging she walked back toward the men. Gabe loped down the trail. Watching him disappear down the trail, the men were stunned when Feral slipped away and in a moment was gone from sight.

"That damn fool woman, she sure has a big fire in her for Gabe to be so dumb," said Red.

"Better go get her," said Paul. "Can't be saving her and save our own butts."

"Leave her, let Gabe handle her," sneered Red. "She is no fragile chicken, she can take care of herself, damn betcha."

Pushing through the brush, Feral could see the truck and the two rangers looking it over. The copter blades were still, the engine idling. Leaning forward for a better view, her breath caught as a hand went over her mouth and with a quick movement she felt herself wrapped up like a trussed turkey. Struggling, she felt his lips against her ear.

"Quiet," said Gabe. "I told you to stay put."

"Let's steal the copter and make our get away," she said throatily.

"Why didn't you run the other way, go home?" he said relaxing his grip slightly.

"Cause, I'm having fun and I want to see how this whole gig turns out."

"This is no gig. This is bad stuff. No fun at all," murmured Gabe.

She turned slowly around all the while pressed against him. He looked down at her and grinned whispering, "You are feral, a tame thing gone wild."

Pulling his head toward her, she kissed him deeply. His lips softened against hers. Her heart pounded. She rubbed against his chest pulling him closer. She could feel him swell hot between her legs.

Suddenly he let her go and stared over her head at the truck and the rangers. She slumped against him, her legs weak. The rangers were scanning the area with their binoculars as they moved toward the helicopter. The trees rattled as the copter lifted and moved away to the west. Once it was out of sight, they snuck up on the pickup. The hood was lifted. Looking inside they could see that all the wires reachable had been jerked loose or cut.

"This is an asshole thing to do," spit Feral. "How did they know this didn't belong to one of their goddamn sled heads?"

"Look," said Gabe pointing to the jockey box left open with papers spilling out of it, "I'm betting they know whose rig this is and they have gone back for a whole damn army. I can doctor a horse, or track a wolverine, but fixing an engine isn't something I know how to do. Besides, it would take hours and they will be back with the whole damn cavalry by then."

"Paul didn't take his registration out of here?" said Feral. "I've just got to teach you boys some hiding skills. Who knew the Indians were so lousy at this kind of thing. Now I know why you kept ending up on the wrong side of the war. You didn't listen to your women."

Gabe jumped up in the back of the pickup and started opening boxes. "Paul did one thing right, he has a case of oil and a can of gasoline back here. We got a rig back at the cave that might run if it had some of both. Grab that can, I'll carry the oil, we will probably have to come back and get the battery if my truck won't start."

Picking their way through the tall grass, soggy tundra and an occasional small hotpot, they stopped for a breather.

"I hate to bring this up in the midst of your giddy," said Feral, "but your pickup has a 500- pound bear spread out in the back who is not likely to get off or move over or want to hitch another ride, cause he's dead."

"We got that all figured out," said Gabe impatiently, "we just run up the side of a hill and he falls out."

"Do you then back over him," replied Feral batting her eyelashes.

"You think you know everything. Of course, it's always after the fact. Stop buggin me or I will let Red have at you," snapped Gabe.

"Don't ever threaten me with that pig again or I will cut the balls off both of you and boil them for breakfast," she replied.

"For a woman, you got some mouth on you," said Gabe.

"I am no shrinking violet that is true enough. As to my mouth," she smirked, "I felt parts of you enjoying it a moment ago."

Watching the color fill his face, Feral laughed. "You are something sweet, Tonto."

"Don't call me that," he said.

For a moment Feral studied him, watching his eyes blacken, his chin thrust forward. She liked it better when he was blushing. "I'm sorry. Just teasing." Silent, they filed down the trail toward the cave.

"I'm gonna point the nose straight at the embankment and gun it hard," said Gabe. "You all get in the back and push him out. Feral, you stay back, cause when this bad ass comes off the back of this pickup, he's landing hard."

Jake finished pouring the gas in the tank, screwed the gas can cap on and tossed the can in the bushes. Feral, with a disgusted look, picked it up.

"You might just need this. What happened to all the Indians who knew how to get along in the wild? You guys are a bunch of morons. It's a damn good thing I am here."

"Oh, yea," said Red, "ole Red sure needs some old broad to set me straight." Feral, holding the gas can, threw it at Red. Paul caught it mid-air. Red laughed.

"You have one short fuse, lady," said Paul. "You are scaring me more than the Feds."

"Mind if I get a little help here," said Gabe leaning out the truck door. Blue smoke poured out of the exhaust pipe. "This guy's a heavy load, I need you all to push. The tires are sunk down in the muck."

Lining up on either side and behind, they pushed the pickup out of the rut and started it moving toward the steep bank. Revving the engine, Gabe put it in low gear, punched the gas pedal and with a shake like a bull getting ready to charge it moved forward. At the bottom of the cliff the truck made a tentative lurch up the grade and then died. Rolling back down, Gabe waited until it came to stop, ground on the starter and got it going again. The crew lined up again.

"Get away from the back end," yelled Gabe motioning to Jake.

Red hollared "Stay where you are. We need somebody to catch him."

With a glare at Red, Jake walked nonchalantly around the side toward the cab, his ears burning red. Ramming the truck up the steep incline with Red, Jake, Paul and Feral pushing and yelling encouragement, Gabe watched in his rear view mirror waiting for the bear to fall out. No go. The bruin seemed stuck with superglue to the bed of the truck.

"Get in the back and push him out," yelled Gabe.

"Nah, I ain't getting that close," said Red. "I'll drive, you push."

"It's my pickup," said Gabe, "and you stink about as bad as that bear."

"It's not the stink man. Its bad medicine for a Blackfeet to piss off the grizzly spirit."

"You're saying it's a cultural thing," laughed Feral, "what a crock."

"You know from nothing, woman when it comes to Indians. All you know is you got the hots for our boy Gabe," cracked Red. "You don't know our spirit animals. You don't know our dreams. You are just a wanna be."

"Hey I don't wanna be anything. You been hanging out with tourists too much," said Feral.

"Him being Indian has nothing to do with fucking." At that, all the men looked down at their feet. "It's funny," Feral continued, "you guys are all sass when a woman acts up, but mention sex and you get all dry mouthed and red faced – ah, more red in the face." Climbing in the back, she said "Are we going to dump this load or not?"

Bracing themselves against the cab, they pushed with their feet as Gabe made another run up the embankment. Red stayed on the ground.

"Grab his feet and pull dammit," Jake yelled at Red.

Red shifted his eyes around like he was scouting for signs, then he grabbed a huge paw and jerked. Gabe hit the gas. Paul, Jake and Feral shoved at the huge carcass. Suddenly the bear came loose and with a whoosh, landed on the ground with a thud. The paw still held by Red raked down his cheek leaving bloody tracks. Jumping back, he slipped on the ice and landed on his back next to the bear.

For a moment, everyone just stared. Red lay still, glancing furtively over at the bear like a cornered spaniel, half expecting him to stand up and finish the job. Feral glanced around the group, struck by how serious they all looked. A dozen smart comments drifted into her head. She bit her lip to keep from laughing. Finally, she couldn't take it anymore and tipping her head toward Jake, she whispered, "Red looks like fresh kill game waiting to be skinned, quartered and packaged." Jake's head jerked toward her and then back again to stare at the bear and Red. He grinned.

Finally, Red scrambled to his feet, brushed off his jacket and pants with a sideways glance back at the bear, hurried around to the other side of the truck. Gabe jerked the wheel to turn the truck heading away from the cliff, the bear leaving no room to back up. Grunting and pushing, the crew finally got the pickup going the right direction.

Back in the cave, Gabe stuffed supplies in various duffle bags and yelled, "Throw your gear in the back of the pickup and jump in. We gotta get out of here. It's all going downhill quick. Besides Feral's old man and the cops chasing us over the damn snowmobiler, now we got the Feds down on us for bagging a grizzly and hunting elk in a national park. You're kinda right Feral, we just got a knack for setting ourselves up for a hard fall."

"Whoa," said Red, "speak for yourself man. Ole Red didn't

kill no sled head, although I don't know why that's a crime. I just came cause you was having trouble getting the meat back to the tribe. That elk all but jumped in the frying pan."

Dragging their gear out of the cave, they threw it in the pickup and stood around while Gabe started the pickup. Feral jumped in beside him. Cisco cocked one eye at her and shifted to lean against Gabe. Red reached for the door handle and Feral quickly pushed the lock down. Rolling the window down slightly, she whispered, "Try to get in here and I will feed your nuts to the squirrels first chance I get."

Red kicked the door panel and sauntered back to the pickup bed.

It was noon when they finally pulled away from the cave. The temperature was hovering right around zero and the air had the smell of snow in it. Huddled down in the back of the pickup the men exchanged smokes and stories. In the cab, Gabe kept his eyes on the gauges waiting for the oil light to come on and tell him his trusty pony was about to lock up. Feral, for once, seemed subdued. Glancing over at Gabe from lowered eyes she still felt the distance between them from this morning when her remark and his reaction brought on a cold snap. Digging through her backpack she found some crackers and offered one to Cisco. He sniffed it and let it fall to the seat. Gabe picked it up and after looking it over shoved it in his mouth. Cisco let out a whimper.

Reaching across the seat, Feral caressed Gabe's cheek saying, "Hey, I thought that kiss might lead to another."

"Listen to me," he said, staring straight ahead. "You are thinking this is some kind of lark. Bunch of dumb Indians screwing up and you just along for the ride. Well, it's gonna get tough, cold and miserable. Maybe the cops won't know you are in this pickup and they could start shooting. I want you to get out when we hit the highway. The north gate is just about three miles up the road. Somebody is usually there during the day or they will show up eventually."

"Well, what if there isn't anybody there, am I just supposed to freeze to death?" The uncertainty in her eyes belayed her tough tone.

"You aren't afraid to be alone are you?" Gabe snorted. "You and that plow horse have been riding all over this country alone."

"Gabe, I'm not some debutante who is going to fall into a fainting spell or start weeping. I just don't want to be left out here alone in this kind of cold without a horse or a pickup. Let me stay till we hit town, or a ranger station where somebody actually is."

"Shit, lady, before this is over, you are going to wish you had shot me the first day you caught me naked."

"I figure if I hang around you might just get naked again and this time I'll be loaded and waiting for you," smirked Feral.

"What a piece a work you are," Gabe said. "But enough of this kind of talk, I got an oil light flickering."

"Oh great, I think your mangy mutt has given me his fleas," said Feral, pulling her hat off and scratching her head. Her long hair streaked grey and blonde fell to her shoulders. 

"I warned you, you weren't keeping good company," replied Gabe slowing to a stop as he anxiously watched the oil gauge.

##

Old Man twisted in the hardback chair. It had been two hours. Staring out the frost etched windows he could see the grey haze drifting down the sides of the tall bank building across the street. Billings was the only Montana town with a skyline defined by buildings instead of mountains. Sprung out of the prairie, it seemed belligerent about its progress; shied away from urban planning. No gilding the sagebrush here. Survival was its designer. Like the cattle and oil wells that fueled it, Billings had no inclination toward pretty – just function.

Inside, the room was hot. The Indian woman sitting behind the desk turned away from Old Man and spoke quietly into the phone, her voice lilting. She had already pointed out the coffee pot and a tin of cookies, had done her job by him. From behind the door he could hear a murmur of voices and somebody pounding on the table and then, the door pushed opened.

"Come in, the tribal chairs will hear you now," came a voice from inside. Old Man gathered up the buckskin bag holding the tobacco pouches and shuffled through the door toward the long conference table. His body ached from days of hauling meat through the drifts and leaning out of a helicopter to drop it to the stranded people. I'm a man of a thousand walks, he thought to himself, but my words must be strong and sure. The Council must hear me, they are the new warriors, lawyers, their shield – the voices for Gabe and Paul.

CHAPTER 13

# SHOVEL THIS

"Get your bony ass over away from me," snarled Red.

"Quit pushin, I'm shoved back as far as I can go. You got all the blanket," yelled Jake.

Paul wrapped the sleeping bag tighter around himself and tried to ignore the other two jockeying for protection against the wind blowing over the cab of the pickup. Though it was only half-past two in the afternoon, the thin light was fading and with it came a deepening cold. Scanning the borrow pit alongside the road, he counted three dead elk, a buffalo and a moose in a little over 50 miles. Coyotes, maybe wolves had already been feeding at the carcasses. Winterkill possible, but more likely the work of the snowmobilers, he thought. Running game until their lungs frosted, burst and they choked to death on their own blood was fair game in their twisted minds. Driving by an interpretive sign, he read out loud, "Created as a Pleasuring Ground for the Generations, 1860," the epitaph was etched in the stone entrance to Yellowstone. "Where is the pleasure for who!" he shouted at his companions. They stopped their bickering and cupped their ears indicating they could not hear. Paul shrugged and went back to scanning the ditch as they sped through the twilight. His breath was freezing on his face, his fingers long since had lost their feeling. How did he get himself in this mess anyway.

"Why," Red muttered, "does that damn dog get to ride inside and here I am freezing my ass off. And I don't mean that bitch she dog, although a little fresh air might just settle

her some." Pounding on the cab back window, he motioned for them to pull over.

Easing over on the shoulder, Gabe rolled down the window and hollered out, "What's ya want?"

"I want to change places with the dog," yelled Red.

"Not yet," said Gabe rolling up the window and stepping on the gas. Through the frost, Red could just make out the dog's tongue as he panted in the warmth of the cab. Feral turned around and smirked at him through the window. With a roar, Red grabbed the tire iron from the truck bed and swung it against the window. The glass shattered but did not break through.

Gabe slammed on the brakes - the pickup did a 180. Gabe jumped out of the cab and reached in the back grabbing Red by the front of his jacket. Dragging him toward the tailgate, Red fell to his knees cussing with his arms flailing. Gabe ducking each swing hit the tail gate latch with his free hand. Just as Red hit the ground, Gabe landed a punch right in his face.

"Damn, that hurt my hand," cursed Gabe. Red lay there in the snow, his nose streaming blood. Reaching inside his jacket, he felt the knife in its scabbard and slowly drew it out. Rolling over and slowly getting to his knees, he stared up at Gabe, who was bent over rubbing his hand with snow. Suddenly Red lunged at Gabe with the knife. Then all the air went out of him as he caught a glimpse of Feral on the business end of a shovel. She hit him again, square in the middle, knocking him back. The knife flew out of his hand landing at her feet. Feral leaned on the shovel and looked down at him. "Doesn't seem worth burying." Cisco stood over him snarling.

"In the old days, you would be dragged through camp behind a horse," whispered Red, his stomach and ribs throbbing, "and left to die." Feral tossed the shovel in the pickup bed and jumped in the cab slamming the door.

"I'm thinking about leaving you right where you lay," said Gabe turning toward the truck. Paul threw him a startled look. Jake grinned, his face a frosty pallor. Paul scrambled out of the pickup bed and stood behind Red who lay spread eagle in the snow. Gabe sat in the pickup idling the motor looking back through his rear view mirror. Paul was trying to rouse Red, get him to sit up. But Red just laid there moaning and cursing his nose streaming blood.

"Hey, man, let him stew awhile," said Jake. "He's had no mercy for any of us. I'm glad she took after him with the shovel. Should have shoved the handle where the sun don't shine," he added wryly.

Paul grabbed Red underneath his shoulders and dragged him toward the truck. Red struggled to get loose and with a jerk fell to his side. Groaning, he struggled to his feet and rolled into the back of the pickup. Grabbing the sleeping bag and wrapping it around him he said, his voice ragged, "No Blackfeet warrior is going to be helped up like an old woman."

The road they followed led deeper into the Park toward Old Faithful and away from the main highway. It had been carved by snow machines Gabe noted wryly. Flanking the

roadside ditch a small herd of buffalo stood their coats glazed with ice, their great heads sweeping the snow away from the patches of brown grass, seemingly oblivious to the travelers.

"They look cold," said Feral as she continued to scratch at her head. She shivered more from the idea of fleas jumping on her from Cisco than from the temperature inside the cab. Cisco watched her, every once in a while scratching himself. Feral felt certain the dog was enjoying her itch. Cisco liked having Gabe to himself.

"That ice buildup is a good sign," commented Gabe. "Their hides are so thick with layers of fat and hair that no heat escapes to melt it. There is nothing warmer than a buffalo robe. It's transfusion time to the transmission," said Gabe pulling over to the shoulder.

"I'm thinking we might want to invite one of them fuzzy buffs right back here, crawl right next to him," said Paul as he passed the cans of oil to Gabe. Red stared at him, hatred hardening his black eyes.

As if the buffalo had decided to think it over, they clambered up the bank and starting milling around the pickup. Feral felt her heart begin to pound. These are huge animals and if they decided to stomp this pickup, they could. She remembered a story about an old bull who didn't like the color yellow and he would crush it whether it was a dandelion or a motor vehicle. A couple of winters ago, a skier driving his yellow VW bug was stopped by the old baron right in the middle of road. The bull then proceeded to hook the top of the bug with his horn and like a can opener peel the top back. Stuck that horn right in the side of the car roof and strolled around the car ripping metal like fabric. The terrified skier jumped to the other seat as the horn grazed the driver's side. Having created a convertible, the old boy ambled away. His work here was done.

Feral checked out the color of the pickup – white, well, gritty grey now and wondered if ole Yeller hater was hanging out with this crowd. She hunched down in the seat. Cisco woke up, looked around at the converging buffalo and threw himself in a frenzy barking at the closed window. Spittle specked the glass, her jacket and then she felt it on her cheek. "Shut your face, you miserable cur," she yelled pulling on his collar. He turned to her with a snarl. "Wait a minute, you ain't the head of this pack, buddy," she said grabbing his muzzle and squeezing hard. His threatening eyes turned startled then, passive. She held his gaze. “Don’t be giving me your shit anymore. If I want to hump your owner you look the other way.” Cisco lay down on the seat, his head between his paws. She bitch had won and he knew it.

Gabe hurriedly added oil keeping an eye on the buffalo as they crowded closer. They seemed in a stupor, moving heavy and slow, conserving their energy against the deepening cold. The last thin rays of the setting sun cast a blue haze against the snow. Soon it would be dark. Gabe slammed the hood and tossed the oil can in the back. Only the mounds of sleeping bags let him know his passengers hadn’t bailed out. Better find a way to warm them up, he thought. Better get Red’s knife away from him. The road was deserted. They were the only ones in this cold world.

##

Cigarette smoke haze filled the room. Styrofoam coffee cups and the remains of a sheet cake, its blue icing glowing in the florescent lights, littered the table along with stacks of newspapers. One lone woman sat with the ten other tribal chairmen.

Old Man sat down, looked around the circle and said, “You, our leaders, speak for Indian people on all reservations. Sure, Paul Heavy Shield and Gabe Dumont are from Blackfeet Country, your country,” he said nodding to man sitting at the north end of the table. But we are all Indian People.

“The Park Service got no respect for our traditional hunting ways, the white snowmobilers get their fun from tormenting our buffalo–running them in deep snow till the cold freezes in their lungs. Paul and Gabe stopped them to save the buffalo and you see what happens. Facts are twisted, stories told that will put our warriors in jail for something that was done in honor." He looked straight ahead seemly through the walls of the room to the winter day coating the grey sky. Tapping out each word with his fingers on the table top, he said, "We must come forward and speak on their behalf. Gather your tribal attorneys together, let them come out with a battle plan. Paul and Gabe are hiding in Yellowstone Park. It's cold, they can't stay there. White man's court dates will be set. Paul and Gabe will be hunted down. Rounded up like the buffalo at the end of a rifle. Run to ground like our people were."

##

The tapping on the back window grew more insistent. Feral swung her head around, Gabe looked back through his rear view mirror. Paul's face appeared ghostly with frost tinging his eye lashes and coating his checks. He gestured to pull over, his movements slow.

Gabe eased the pickup over to the shoulder watching to see he didn't end up off the road into the deep embankment.

"Hey, man, it's just too cold back here. I can't feel my feet," Paul's teeth chattered through the words. "We have to stop, warm up."

Off in the distance they could see several dim lights. And like insects, the high pitched whine of a snow machine carried through the gloom.

"Seems we have stopped on the snow machine thoroughfare," said Feral, leaning out the window and pointing to a parking lot just across the way. Adjusting their eyes to the flat landscape, they could make out a few trucks with trailers parked among the stubby pine trees, but no buildings.

"Gabe," said Feral, "my ranch is only about ten miles from here, just before Old Faithful and you can get there on a back road. We could go there now and get you more supplies and you could unload your unwanted baggage – me. Just make sure you take Red when you leave."

"What's you gonna tell your old man? Bet he's got the state patrol looking for you right now," said Gabe.

"There are some outbuildings, an old bunkhouse we only use during branding. You could hide there for a day or so, not long, but everybody could get warm."

"What about the smoke from the stove? He will see it."

"Okay, this is the deal, my dad lives in town during the winter chasing some skirt in Big Timber. He won't be out until it thaws. I'm out there mostly alone, a fact I didn't want you guys to know. The only one who comes around is the rancher from the next place who helps me feed cattle once a day."

"So why the bunkhouse, why not your bed," said Gabe rubbing his hand along her thigh.

"Cause I got nosy neighbors. I got a gentleman caller, but maybe," she smirked.

Gabe jumped out of the pickup, the snow crunched beneath

his boots. It is cold, he thought, I better get them in where there's a fire real damn quick. They still had that ten miles to Feral's ranch. Nudging Paul, Gabe told him the plan to go to Feral's place. Paul nodded slowly, his voice slurred. Walking around the pickup, he patted each man to see if he could get a response, Red's black-eyed glare was his only message.

Jerking open the door on Feral's side, he pulled her out and held her against him. Tipping her chin up, he said, "Your turn to ride in the back and take the dog with you. He will keep you warm. Those guys aren't gonna make another 10 miles." She started to protest, but Gabe spun her around, called to Cisco and walked them both back to the tailgate. "Okay guys, can't feel your parts anymore, get in the cab." Paul and Jake crawled toward him. Swinging his legs over the side, Paul pushed off and fell to his knees in the snow.

"I can't feel my legs, man," he slurred. Gabe pulled him up and began to briskly rub his legs. Paul yelped as the circulation stung.

"Stomp your feet if you want to keep them," Gabe ordered. "Why weren't you moving around back here, did you forget everything in Seattle?"

Jake climbed slowly out of his sleeping bag, beating life back in his sluggish limbs. Red stared at them, blood from his broken nose froze in trickles down his chin, black circled his swollen eyes. Hunched in his bag he shook his head. "Not gonna ride close up with you prick."

"Then stay back here and freeze your balls off, I don't give a damn," said Gabe.

"I'm not sitting back here with him," said Feral.

"Then I guess you walk. I'm driving until one of you shows some sign of life that you can keep the truck on the road. Then I'll take my turn back here."

"I'll wait," snarled Red.

"Suit yourself," snapped Gabe.

Feral climbed into the back and grabbed the shovel. Leaning toward Red, she said, "Remember where this fit before? If you come anywhere near me, I'll do my damn best to bash in your skull. Don't even look my direction."

Red stared out at her the bag covering everything but his bloody nose and black rimmed eyes. "I got time just wait," he sneered. Cisco looked from one to the other and seeing no comfort, slunk over to the corner and curled in a ball.

Inside the cab, Paul and Jake squirmed as the circulation stung their legs like feet pins and needles.

"What's the plan, man?" said Jake, his teeth chattering. Frostbite painted white patches on his cheeks.

Gabe tried to sound confident as he laid out their next move. Between watching the gas tank needle dip lower and waiting for the oil light to come back on, he felt his spirits slip. What a mess. How had something that started out as a way to feed hungry people get them in such a way.

A dark crimson brushed the snow as the sun set behind the mountain. Suddenly it was colder and visibility was rapidly fading. Feral tapped on the window and beckoned for Gabe to turn on the side road. The truck hit a rut and Feral fell forward on her knees her face inches from Red's. Hatred heated the distance between and she quickly back away. Red licked his cracked lips and snickered.

Silver Ridge Ranch was the only privately owned property in Yellowstone Park. It was there before there was a park and had passed through the family to Feral's mother. After her death from cancer one year ago, Feral's father was considering selling it to a very rich New Yorker. The Park was after it as the development potential posed a real threat to the natural environment.

Feral had grown up on the ranch but went away to the city for college and stayed there twenty-years. She wanted it but she had no real money. Writers barely eke out a living. And now with the divorce she was really on her own.

Tapping on the window, Feral motioned for Gabe to change places with her. He had found the turn off but the road constantly forked to keep Park visitors confused and away from the ranch.

Slowing to a stop, Gabe helped her out of the back and cautioned her to keep an eye on the gauges. He climbed in the pickup bed and pulled Cisco over to him and wrapped them both in a sleeping bag. Red watched from hooded eyes. Feral gunned the pickup forward, Gabe flinched and muttered. "Hey, no rough ridin'."

The trees pressed in, the moon lost from view and inside the cab there was silence. Both men were still shaking with cold and wondering if this wild woman really was going to do them some good. So far, it had been nothing but bad.

Feral scrapped the windshield as she drove. Glancing over at her two passengers, she declared that they were as worthless as teats on a boar. For once nobody rose to the challenge. They figured she could say anything she wanted as long as she kept driving toward a warm fire. She considered heaping piles of just plain rotten comments on them just to see if they were still kicking, but then, she had to drive. And scrape.

Gabe jumped out and pushed open the garage door. Nudging the pickup inside, Feral turned off the engine and with a wave of her arm she led the way to the main farmhouse. Lights in the window promised heat and comfort and food. Jerking open the front door, she could make out her neighbor Sam sitting at the kitchen table drinking coffee. Feral blocked the door and with a whisper, told the men to go back to the garage until she got rid of him. Groaning, they retraced their steps.

"Sam, never doubt my hospitality, but why are you here, didn't see your rig outside."

Sam quickly crossed the distance between them and grabbing her shoulder, said, "You scared the bejezzus out of me. Your horse showed up an hour ago when I was feeding cattle. Figured I'd give you to about now to call out the search. What happened?"

Feral could hear Cisco scratching at the door and whining. Taking off her jacket and boots she said, "I was riding out near the ranger station when a helicopter flew overhead and buzzed us. Buckets blew up and took off. I hit the snow. One of the rangers lent me his pickup till tomorrow. My butt hurts but that's all. Deep snow."

"Sure you are okay?" Sam's blue eyes took stock from her boots on up.

"Yea, I am going to get in the tub, then hit the sack. Appreciate you waiting here and worrying."

"Okay then, I will check on you tomorrow, usual time. I put Buckets in the barn. He's good for tonight."

"Thanks again, Sam. You are a good neighbor." Feral hoped the hurry didn't show in her voice. Had to get those guys out of that cold garage or hang 'em up for meat.

Watching from the window, she watched Sam ride out of sight. Running down the icy path to the garage she was met by the pathetic trio beating their limbs trying to force enough life in them to walk the distance to the house. For once, Feral kept her thoughts to herself.

Feral scrambled some eggs, but the exhausted men lay sprawled on the living room sofa, chair and on the floor in front of the fireplace, too tired to eat. With just her there during the week, there wasn't a lot of fresh food in the house. Of course the freezer was full of beef, deer and elk, but the only thawing going on was in the living room. Tossing them pillows and blankets, she told them they could heat up the bunkhouse tomorrow. They didn't even move.

Soaking in the tub, she listened for Gabe. She was beginning to feel put out. Gabe had barely spoken to her since her “Tonto” remark, as if that was a big friggin deal. He was probably a smuck when it came to women especially ones who knew their own mind. Her ex-husband didn’t have any staying power either. Said she wore him out. She could pull back on the throttle but then who would she be? She felt pretty righteous lying there in the bubbles, after all, those four bozo’s have her to thank. Never seen such incompetent Indians. Worse than tourists. Chuckling to herself, she sank down in the water, holding her nose. The warm water tingled her scalp, her thoughts free floated, her shoulders and neck let go of today.

Feeling a chill, she sat up and opened her eyes. Sitting on the toilet drinking a beer, Red leered at her, his blood-shot red eyes inches from hers. For a moment she felt paralyzed. Then she screamed. With a glance toward the bathroom door, Red reached over to cover her mouth grabbed a hand full of hair and pulled her head back. Feral’s eyes darted. Did she have no heroes? Were those ungrateful lugs just going to sleep?

Bringing his face close to hers, Red let go of her hair and with a snicker said, “Where’s your hot shot when you need him? Guess it’s up to ole Red to take care of the women – like always.” With that he let go of her, turned and left.

Hurrying to bed, she grabbed the shotgun off the rack in the hallway. She half hoped Red would come into her bedroom so she’d have a reason to plug him. Glancing in the living room she could see all four sleeping like there was no tomorrow. Better keep them in the house so her neighbor didn’t see the bunkhouse chimney smoke and start wondering.

CHAPTER 14

# THIS WAY OR THEIR WAY

Old Man sat quiet. He had told the story to the council tribal chairmen of how Paul and Gabe had tried to save the buffalo herd and in doing so, were now the hunted ones. Louie Looking Horse, a young council attorney, spoke first. "Paul skipped on his bail, didn't appear at his hearing. If we are to command our place in the white man's court, then we have to play by their rules so that we are the clear victor. Paul and Gabe need to come in."

The Lakota Sioux chairman began to drum his fingers on the table. Soon all eyes in the room turned to him as he spoke. "Our people share the same spirit with Tatanka. Buffalo are human beings, our people. For thousands of years they cared for us, now we must come for them, bring them home. This is not just about white man's court or even our brave warriors who began our fight. Now is the time for us to act. Too long the buffalo have been held hostage to the government system while our people lose spirit."

Looking Horse waited for the elder to finish, the only reflection of impatience was the tick in his cheek. "I see only the surface of the stream," he said, "not the deep pool from where your wisdom comes. The courts are the battlefield of the Feds. That is where our warriors must make their stand. I say again, Paul and Gabe have to come in. We cannot defend a shadow. White judges must see and hear what's in their heart."

Some of the members of the Council nodded in agreement, others shrugged, their eyes shifting away. No words were spoken.

Taking a long sip of his lukewarm coffee, the chairman looked to Old Man. "You go to the warriors and tell them what you hear at this council. Let each one decide. It is our way."

As Old Man made his way from the building, Louie Looking Horse met him on the sidewalk. Wearing only a light shirt, he seemed oblivious to the cold wind, his body burning with determination.

"I respect chairman's words, but the way of this world is through the court system. This is where we will win our most honored battles today. Tell Gabe and Paul that hiding will only get them a shorter rope. I have spent many years learning the system and I say to you, they cannot stay gone long enough to be free."

Old Man patted him on the arm, his smile was one for a willful boy. "I will bring the words of the council and our warriors will decide whether to stand their ground where they are or come to you. They will choose. It is our way."

Watching Old Man shuffle down the street, Louie felt the twitch in his jaw tighten.

##

Red gripped the telephone tightly willing Lucy to answer. He knew if the others saw him, all hell would break loose. Hearing the answering machine click on, he muttered, "Those fuckers forget that we are not packing the same load. I didn't run over the sled head." Lucy's voice assured him that

she would get right back to him if he left his name and number. A quick "I'm okay," and he hung up the phone. Feral stood blocking the doorway, her arms crossed, a hardened glint in her eye.

"You really are a dumb son-of-a-bitch aren't you? Might as well called the cops directly. They will trace that line to here. And by the way," she snarled as he brushed past her, "next time you come at me, you'll be the one coming up for air."

While Feral fed the cows with her neighbor Sam, Gabe and Paul talked about their next move. Jake sprawled on the sofa, his long legs hanging over the end. Hoisting himself up on one elbow, he reminded them that he had best be getting along. After all, he had only been along for the ride. Hadn't killed anybody, no hunting in the Park, why, he could even claim he'd most likely saved that miserable Kenny's life by driving him into town. The more he thought about it, the more confident he felt that he would be welcomed back by all with a great story to tell. He just needed the pickup. Gabe and Paul let him rave for a couple of minutes, then they continued their discussion.

Feral stomped her boots in the mud room, lashes frosty and cheeks red. Red met her in the kitchen and handed her a cup of coffee. She looked at it and then at him, walked to the sink and poured it down the drain. Turning around, she said, "What do you want?"

"To get out of here. Ole Red here ain't responsible for all this crap. I just liberated some meat. Red didn't take out the sled head or the griz. The elk, well, it was okay, we were hungry and they got lots of them."

"What's stopping you? You sure as hell won't be missed by anybody here." Feral's voice was cold.

"I need a rig and Gabe's truck is I D 'd all over the news. That Tribal Fish & Game emblem on the door is a bull's eye. Drive it and I'm screwed," said Red.

"So, why you tell me, do you really think I would help your lame ass in anyway?"

"You wanna get rid of ole Red. I'm guessin you don't much like me."

Feral snorted. "What's to like? If I lend you my Blazer you are going to have to say you stole it. Course I know that will give you trouble, but auto theft will be the least of your worries. Do you understand that you have aided and abetted criminals? The very ones sitting in the living room plotting their next major mistake."

"What about you, she cat." Red's eyes were now black, blue and yellow where the bruising had spread. He looked like he was painted for battle. "You are up to your tittys in Gabe's mess. How about a deal, you won't tell on ole Red and I don't know you from a hole in the ground."

"Let me think about it."

"While you're thinking, Red could be high tailin' it outa your life, lady."

"Don't push it," she said. Grabbing the coffee pot, Feral kept her eyes on Red as she pushed around him. Just as she reached the door, Red reached over and patted her butt. For a second she hesitated, shocked in spite of herself. Spinning around, she hit him full force with the hotpot spilling coffee down his chest.

"Call a cab." Feral went to the living room still carrying the coffee pot. All three men held up their mugs for a refill. "Red's wearing it."

Missing her meaning, Jake yelled, "That badger always gets his first."

Looking out the window, Paul could see Red ducking around buildings, glancing furtively back at the house. "I do believe our Blackfeet brother is planning a coup. I just bet he's going to steal one of our rusty steeds."

"Let em' go," said Gabe.

"Hey, he can't just take off. How am I gonna get out of here," yelled Jake making a dash out the door. Waving his arms and yelling, Jake watched in frustration as the blue Blazer raced by kicking up snow and gravel. Watching it disappear into the trees, he was suddenly conscious of how cold he was. Looking down, he realized he didn't have any shoes or jacket on. His socks were sticking to the ice. Shoulders slumped and socks picking up snow, he limped back to the house.

Inside all eyes were tuned to the television. On the screen buffalo were being shot by park rangers outside Yellowstone's boundaries. The newscaster recounted the fact that to date over one third of the herd, 1,093 buffalo, had been shot or slaughtered. The camera switched to five people who had chained themselves to a Park Service pickup protesting the handling of the bison issue. A local rancher shouted at the protestors that buffalo carry Brucellosis to cattle. His livelihood was in danger, he grumbled to the reporter, but these tree huggers didn't care about that. Never mind that they had beef for supper and wore leather shoes.

The next scene was Billy and Leroy in jail. Then photos of Paul and Gabe. The newscaster reported that Paul's truck had been found inside the gates of Yellowstone Park and they had reason to believe that the fugitives were hiding somewhere in the Park.

"No mention of the bear or the elk carcass, probably haven't found the cave yet," said Gabe.

*"Questioning of the men held in custody continues in this bizarre case with few clues as to the whereabouts of Gabe Dumont and Paul Heavy Shield,"* continued the newscaster. *"Leroy LaRue, one of the men involved in the original altercation, is currently held at the county jail in Billings. He insists that the whole situation was a rescue mission of the buffalo herd from the snow machine drivers. He claimed they took the injured rider to the hospital but had no involvement in his injuries. Billy Sioux claims to have no knowledge of the clash between the tribal members and the sledders at the site of the conflict, but states his role was to take the buffalo meat from the game station where it was held by the Park Service and distribute it to the tribes. With Skip Johnson in critical condition, one of the two men on the snow mobiles, the fact that the suspects are American Indian and that the alleged crime took place in a national park has brought in the FBI. It is unknown at this point who exactly is responsible for the injury to Johnson. The story has been picked up by the national wire service and it is expected to generate controversy over the buffalo issue and the tribe's petition to distribute the live bison that leave the Park to the reservations. The search for Gabe Dumont and Paul Heavy Shield continues."*

"All trails will eventually, if not sooner, lead here," said Feral switching off the television. "While it's great to be rid of that asshole Red you know he'll save his hide over yours if he gets cornered. Besides, he made a phone call from here so they will trace it."

As the afternoon began to fade into darkness the three men stared at the flames dimming as the logs burned out. Breaking the silence, Paul said, "Let's remember what is really at stake here. This isn't just about us."

CHAPTER 15

# THEY COME AND THEY GO

Lucy's heart began to pound as she heard Red's voice on her answering machine. She wondered how much trouble he was in now. How mixed up was he in the injury of the snow machine driver? She knew Red was a hot head with big mouth. "Hope the only thing he shot off was his mouth," she murmured grimly.

If only Old Man would let her know where they were, but she also knew he would tell her nothing. He had not forgiven her for going to Red after Paul left. Ten years was long enough to wait for a man who was still looking for his place in the world.

Throwing some venison, potatoes and onions in a pot, she

decided to cook just in case Red came home today. Adjusting the flame under the stew she heard a scuffle at the door. Calling Red's name, she rushed to open it. A blast of cold air and the pistol leveled at her head pushed her back. "Seems we are interested in seeing the same guy," sneered the agent. "We'll just wait together."

##

Red grinned as he gunned the engine and spun onto the highway. "Hot damn, good to be rid of them sorry sons-a-bitches and their sled head problems." A state patrol car passed him going 70 mph. Smart trick taking this Blazer he thought. Nobody gonna be looking for this rig. He'd see his woman, his Lucy, by midnight if the weather held. Rocking side to side, he reached in his back pocket, pulled out a can of tobacco and stuck a wad in his cheek. Get a pack of cigarettes at the first quick stop he thought. Pack of cigarettes and a six pack. Lay in travel supplies. He grinned and added a quart of whiskey to his list.

##

Feral turned the steaks on the stove grill. "This could be the last supper," she muttered.

Jake opened the oven and poked the potatoes.

"Can you stop with the pokin'? That's the third time in the last half-hour. Lets all the heat out" said Gabe.

"I'm hungry," said Jake. He dipped a finger in the corn simmering on the stove.

Feral stuck him with her long handled fork. "Right through your spleen, skewered and served rare."

"You are one hostile woman," said Jake jumping back. "What did you do to your old man? Did you scare him off, or is he buried here? Are you keeping him in the freezer? Maybe that's him what we are eating for supper," chortled Jake.

"Don't you worry none, you aren't fit for cooking," said Feral.

Gabe paced back and forth in front of the fireplace, squatting down now and then to adjust the log or just stare into the flames. He knew they should turn themselves in just as he knew they could languish in jail a long time. The truth was they hadn't hurt anyone, but the facts all pointed that way. What they needed was time, time and a safe place to tell their side of the story. How would they get that if they had to rely on white man's court, especially with the FBI involved.

The FBI was still looking to get even over Wounded Knee from the 1970's, the one time Indian power rose up during the Civil Rights Movement. And then there was the time we occupied the federal building in DC, he thought grimacing. He had been both places with his parents. And in the end, what was left was a reservation all shot to hell, two dead agents and one Indian serving time. Still not enough blood for the government. Never mind the tribal members who died at Wounded Knee. Nobody counted them. Just like nobody would see that the other snow machine ran over the driver.

He wished there were more of his people right here, right now. Really, it is just Paul and me, he thought. Jake will cut and run at the first chance. He's got no convictions and no backbone. A safe place where they could be heard, that's what they needed. He hoped Paul was right about his dream showing them traveling inside the Park to the lodges. In the vision, Paul saw Gabe holding a torch while their people gathered outside chanting for him to burn the buildings down. Outside the circle, the soldiers stood with their rifles pointed, but no shots rang out.

Would it work? he wondered. How many buildings in ashes before the government would hear? Should they start or end with Old Faithful? Was burning the white man's sacred monument worse than killing a man? Gabe thought maybe yes, but how else would the Feds stop to hear the truth. Listen to him. Hear the stories of his people starving on the barren reservations. Paul and he would leave in the morning. Jake was on his own.

In the kitchen, Feral told Paul she didn't understand why his people were so unhappy with their lot, so unproductive. "Aren't they given money, food, housing and healthcare? Sounds like a sweet deal to me," she said.

Paul sighed, so many whites believed that. Because of the treaties the government had to provide some welfare, but people were still dying from the effects of poor nutrition from the starchy government rations. Farming was not a cultural fit for tribes that had a nomadic history. The land discarded by whites as poor quality was held in trust by the Feds so most of his people could not own the land they lived on. They stayed anyway, counting on family ties to stay strong. They didn't fit outside the rez, but the reservations are red ghettos. No way to leave, no place to go. If native people went back to their ancestral land, to the wild places, if they could live with the buffalo, they would find that hope, that purpose. They would finally be home.

It was still two hours before dawn when they loaded supplies on the snow machines. Paul and Gabe had let out a howl when Feral told them snow machines were their only choice. Red had taken her blazer, Gabe's truck had a steady oil leak and by using the sleds they could stay off the roads. It was that or snowshoes and carrying a fifty-pound pack for 20 miles.

"Hot damn, I gotta admit this is a kick," Gabe said, as he gunned the machine in a circle around the yard. "Never been on one before."

Paul looked leery as Feral explained the gears and braking system. Jake stood in the doorway watching. Finally, the sleds were loaded and the guys tied down their loads.

Feral yelled over to Jake, "Which one are you climbing on?

"I'm not goin'," said Jake backing further into the doorway.

"Oh yes you are," said Feral striding toward him. "I am out of vehicles and just so you know, I am going to call the cops to report a stolen Blazer once you are all well down the road. If I don't, then it is my ass as well."

"You're turning us in," yelled Jake.

"Yes. My story is that I provided shelter for some guys that claimed car trouble and one of them stole my Blazer. Paul and Gabe cooked it up last night and it works for me. Otherwise I am aiding and abetting. That's not the thanks I was looking forward to."



Gabe revved the engine, black smoke tinged the crisp air. "You wanna walk?"

"Jake, you can hitch a ride out of Old Faithful easier than here," said Paul. "Get on with me, I'm going to take it pretty slow and I got more room."

"I go, I drive," said Jake. "I rode these before."

"Ridden or driven?" said Feral.

"No matter," said Paul quickly, "he can drive, I'm okay."

Jake reappeared with his pack and traded places with Paul.

"It's like a bronc that just needs a steady hand," said Gabe gunning the engine.

Paul settled on the back and gingerly grasped Jake around the middle. "Better hang on tighter than that. I ain't looking behind to pick you up."

Feral watched them from the window until the smoke from the engines was gone. Give them three or four hours, she thought, then call the cops. She could always claim she was sleeping when the Blazer left and didn't discover it until today.

First it was the red streaked sky turning to a golden hue that painted the snow and the mountain tops that made them stop their machines in wonder. They had followed the Gallatin River to where it became a lake. Twenty or more Trumpeter Swans, their wing span spreading over seven feet, glided along the frozen surface finally settling on the opposite shore. Their white plumage blended into the snow banks. With regret, they started up the noisy machines and continued on. When automobiles first showed up in the West, the Indians called them "skunk wagons." Snow mobiles were worse.

Feral had warned them to stay west of Mammoth Hot Springs because that lodge had been winterized and the road leading right to the door was open all winter. Even though it wasn't the weekend it was bound to have skiers and more sledders. At Madison Lake, they turned east to follow Obsidian Creek. Following the stream bottoms, while it was brushier and the downed trees made navigating harder, it kept them from having to climb the mountain passes where the ceaseless wind drifted the snow and the temperature dropped hard. In some places, rock outcroppings threatened to high-center the snow machines. The constant jarring and engine noise dulled their minds.

Most of the thermal areas were dormant, but they kept a close eye out for plumes of vapor which meant active hotpots with unstable ground.

Mid-morning, Gabe waved for them to pull over. "We are coming up on Norris. It's closed now, but according to Feral, it is the halfway point to Old Faithful and folks usually stop there. We need to stay out of sight."

"Not me," said Jake stomping his feet to get the circulation going. "I might get me a ride."

"Have at it," said Gabe shrugging his shoulders.

"What if you don't?" said Paul. "The folks coming in here are on skis or sleds and there won't be room for you. Besides, how are you going to explain being here without any way to get here?  Try telling that to a Park ranger."

Jake shifted his weight and looked from Paul to Gabe. Gabe leaned against a rock warmed by the sun and yawned. He wondered how they would start this whole thing off. It seemed kind of crazy to hole up in Old Faithful if nobody knew. The torch should be lit when they sent word or he and Paul would be over-run immediately. Who would carry the message?

"Man, I just can't shake loose," said Jake climbing back on the machine. Steamboat, the world's tallest geyser, stood silent.

##

Red heaved a heavy sigh as he turned into Lucy's driveway. It had been a hell of a trip, dark, windy and really, really long. "Drove clear across the whole damn state," he muttered as he climbed out of the blazer. His butt was numb and his back was on fire. "Ole Red's too damn old for this all night drivin shit," he muttered.

Walking stiffly up to the front door, he wondered why the lights were on. It was two AM so what was Lucy doing up. She normally went to bed early. As he reached to pull the door open, the light suddenly switched off. "What the hell?" From the corner of his eye he saw the shade move.

Is his woman cheatin'? Has she got somebody in there with her. I'm gonna kill 'em both! Slamming through the door he felt a sharp pain on the back of his head, then all went black. He couldn't bear to open his eyes. The pain throbbing behind his eyelids beat like a rattle. His arms were tingling and numb all at the same time. Struggling to sit up he realized he couldn't. He was trussed like a turkey.

Lucy knelt beside him and stroked his face. He squinted and gave her a half-hearted wink. Hovering above her tear streaked face, stood the skinniest man Red had ever seen. He looked like a razor blade, all sharp edges with his grey eyes, steel rimmed glasses, thin lips and short clipped hair.

As the man shoved his FBI badge in Red's face, he put aside any notions he had about Lucy gone astray. Focusing on the agent, Red said, "Got a smoke for a broken down, tired old Indian?"

"Maybe. Then we talk." Untying one hand, Razor Face, as Red decided to call him, lit a cigarette and placed it between Red's up stretched fingers.

"I gotta pee," said Red. "Can you untie my other hand? You can keep me hobbled like some ole mare if that will make a city boy like you feel more confident."

"You got one hand," said agent, loosening the ropes around his feet and pulling him to his knees. "Use it for your cigarette or your dong." Another push and Red was on his feet with one arm tied securely behind his back.

As Red walked past, the agent stepped in front of him demanding to know why he was all black and blue. "Walked into a door," said Red.

"Was that door slammed in your face by your buddies joy riding around Yellowstone?"

"No buddies of mine."

"So you were in the Park?"

"Never said that," Red slammed the bathroom door shut.

"What do you know about Gabe Dumont and Paul Heavy Shield?"

"Can't a man pee in peace. I've been driving for 12 hours. My bladder is stretched like the hide on a drum."

Shoving open the door, the agent stopped short of knocking Red off balance. "Just checking, don't want you to miss breakfast. Now hurry it up."

Lucy was in the kitchen frying eggs. She and Red had shared a few quiet minutes while the agent talked on his cell phone. He never once turned his back or took his eyes off the couple. Lucy kept apologizing for not warning Red. He whispered questions; why she hadn't yelled out when he reached the door. The agent had two guns, she told him. One pointing at her and one at the door. Was his name mentioned on the news? Did anybody from work call looking for him. Lucy just kept nodding her head no. Then what the hell brought two fisted razor face to his world, he wondered? As the thoughts crossed his mind, Billy the Sioux entered it. I knew, he thought to himself. Billy was a piece of shit the minute he backed down to Pete from Crow rez. Trying to clear his tired brain, Red figured Jake and Billy both had it in for him. Sure, he had given them a bad time, but he was only funnin'. Just like the old days, can't trust a Crow, can't trust a Sioux. "Red was just along for the ride," he mumbled, "no sled head run in, no grizzly, only a measly elk." The FBI better be getting along. He was nothing to them.

Razor face sat at the table picking at his eggs. Red ate with one arm tied fast behind his back and snug to the chair. His eyes felt like a load of gravel had been dumped in them. Rubbing his face, he yelped as his fingers moved across the welts. He couldn't decide who he hated most at this moment, Gabe or Feral. The Feds may not have anything on him, but he might just have a story to tell and that bastard and his bitch be damn sorry before this is over. They'd treated him like a mangy dog. He'd wait. He'd promised Feral he'd get her and by damn, he would. Maybe more ways than one he grinned as he patted Lucy on her butt.

##

By the time the pale sun slid behind the ridge they were bedded down in thick brush. The goulash Feral packed for

them was still hot and they ate quickly scraping the pan. In silence, each man pondered what force of the universe had brought them here. As they lay against the sides of the small tent, the dream, the quest, seemed hazy in the deepening twilight with the cold penetrating their sleeping bags.

Worry edged its way into Gabe's thoughts. He did not have the faith in his people in the way that Paul did. Gabe put his belief in the land. The land would provide if the people were strong and able. He knew the land was good for the people, but were they good to the land. Looking around the reservation at the junked cars and the garbage filled yards, he doubted sometimes.

His folks had fought the battle with the whiskey bottle and lost. He had found his comfort outdoors on their small place with its few poor acres. His horse, a bronc named Moon, bucked him off daily. It taught him to focus, to pay attention or it was more than once a day he'd hit the ground. He loved his dog, Cisco. He named all his dogs Cisco and never knew why. He gentled fawns and once caught a baby black bear until its momma came looking. He was a child, then a man, alone. Only safe in the wild.

His mom and dad, his people, were good, just weak. When they got bucked off, they never climbed back on. Sure there were people on the rez who had built a solid life, but unless they owned their land, they couldn't pass it on. Could his tribe find their hope, their pride if they were in the back country? Would they be afraid? The ones who needed this most, their world was made up of prefab houses and welfare checks. Could they be warriors with only the old stories to lead them? He doubted sometimes. The Pow Wows were not like real life out here, he thought rubbing his cold feet together. The fancy dance garments, like the Ghost Dance ceremony shirts a century ago, would not keep them from danger or from themselves and their weaknesses. None were bullet proof.

Before dawn they had crawled out of their bags and into one of nature's hot tubs. The night had been frigid, the hot water pool was deep enough to cover their shoulders sitting down and it was within running distance of their tent. It was fed by the Firehole River which kept the temperature bearable. Trouble is, these pools could fluctuate several degrees in seconds, so it was important to be very, very alert to change. And to move one's tender balls real quick if things heated up. But right now, all was perfect with the world. A herd of elk moved slowly toward them, drawn by the grass rimming the pools. The guys closed their eyes and relaxed.

"My balls are ready to boil," said Jake, "lets git to getten'."

Gabe figured they'd be at Old Faithful by mid-morning. The thirty miles between Norris and Old Faithful could be crowded with sled heads. They would have to go around Madison which was fed by the West Yellowstone entrance to the park. That town spent big bucks attracting snow machine addicts who bought a lot of beer and drank it on the trails and in motel rooms. Should have traveled by night, he thought, but too many chances to get stuck, high centered or scalded. Besides,

as long as they didn't stop and talk to anyone, they would just be another sled head out to scare the hell out of the wildlife and smoke up the air with dirty exhaust. Just can't be having Jake strike up a conversation before they reach the Lodge.

Traveling through the Lower Geyser Basin between Madison and Old Faithful was tricky. The higher elevation meant less water for the hotpots. These pots burbled and spit mud bubbles, producing fewer plumes of steam making them hard to spot. Jake kept pulling out instead of following Gabe's tracks, doubling the risk. Paul was uneasy with Jake's bravado and was ready to jump and roll.

But just not quick enough. Cresting a small ridge, Jake let out a roar and jerked the machine sharply right just in time to avoid hitting an elk bedded down in the snow. Paul felt himself fall left and getting to all fours, stared into the cow's black eyes. Neither blinked. Jake and Gabe pulled over and slowed their machines to an idle to watch not daring to speak. All around were humps of snow covered elk cows. The bull was nowhere to be seen.

Slowly Paul crawled backwards. Feeling the ground soften under his knees, he turned to look behind him. Just inches away simmered one of those damn bubbling hotpots. Stomped and spit out by an elk herd or cooked in mud. Oh man what a choice thought Paul. The fear of turning his back on the animal paralyzed him. Jake whispered to Gabe that he could just roar over there and grab Paul like a pickup team at a bull riding. Gabe shook his head violently. "Wait," he mouthed. Gabe knew that elk could be dangerous if threatened.

Seconds passed. The elk continued to stare at Paul and Paul at her. Turning to look over at Gabe for help, Paul's fear was visible.

"Stay down, turn sideways and slowly move away," whispered Gabe.

As Paul started to turn, the elk got to her feet and shook. Snow covered Paul making it hard to see. For a moment he froze, then began to move again. Keeping one eye on the beast and one scouting for hotpots, it seemed to take an interminably long time to crawl the 25 feet to his buddies. Watching the rest of the herd come to their feet, their ears cocked alert to danger, Gabe could feel Jake's tension rise along with Paul's and hoped he wouldn't do anything stupid.

Gabe reached down and grabbed Paul's arm pulling him upright. His knees buckled and he sank to the ground. Jake and Gabe dragged him onto the back of the snow machine and hissed "Hang on, we ain't clear yet." Nudging the machines around, the men slowly drove away. Looking back, Paul saw the elk paw the ground and slowly sink back into the snow. No fight today.

Following the Firehole River, they glimpsed the top dormers of Old Faithful Inn framed by the hazy winter sky. Boarded up for the winter, it stood in stark contrast to the tourist season when over two million visitors entered the massive log structure. Now the broad veranda with its massive gnarled tree columns looked cold, unwelcoming, with snow piled up against the door and the lower windows covered with sheets of plywood. Beyond the parking lot and partially hidden by trees, the cabins, stores and gas station had been put to bed for winter. Talk of winterizing the Lodge and opening it to visitors stayed just talk. Working for the Fish and Game Department, Gabe knew money earned at the Park rarely stayed there. Between the concessionaires and the Feds, profits that could be used to take care of these structures went elsewhere. We'll burn a few down, less upkeep, he thought. Turning off the engine, Gabe said, "Bring these machines inside with us, maybe have to make a fast get away."

Digging through the bags attached to the snow machine, they looked for something to pry open the door. "Hope there isn't an alarm system," said Paul.

"Nah," said Gabe as he broke the blade of a screwdriver wedged against the jam and lock. "That wouldn't be friendly and this is America's first national park for all the people. Besides, who would answer it? It's a long haul to the next camp."

"Hey," said Jake, "maybe we leave the front boarded up just to slow 'em down. Bet there is a lot of other places to go through."

"Finally, you show some smarts," said Gabe as he punched Jake's shoulder. Jake glowered at him. "I'm hitting the trail you crazy man with stupid plan."

"Anytime, you go anytime," said Gabe.

Heading in different directions, the trio circled the building looking for an entrance. Hearing a yell, Paul and Jake raced around the side. Looking around, they could not see Gabe only a broad overhang.

"Look up red brothers, look up to where the eagle flies," laughed Gabe. Craning their necks, they could see Gabe on the second story deck. One of the huge glass doors stood open. "Seems somebody left this unlocked for us."

"How'd you get up there?" said Paul.

"Took the stairs, the fire escape. May be damn glad we found it before this is over see as how I ain't planning to roast with the rest."

Leaning over the log railing held up by trunks, their twisted branches forming a three-legged prong, they could see there were two more levels above. Each floor opened to the center – the main room of the building – facing the massive stone fireplace that rose four floors. Huge leaded glass windows provided a back light to the broad walkways and halls leading to the guest rooms. The honey colored wood walls looked warm but froze to the touch. Four chandeliers flanked the fireplace. The silence was complete.

Looking around at the immense structure, to Paul it was more than a white man's building. It was an offering, no matter who it belonged to. The span and grandeur filled one like a forest with towering pines. The hundred-year old structure was still alive with the faint scent of sap. The wood, old before it became the sentry, ribs and arms, carried the memory of the wild. He felt the respect of the creator and those who built it. The master plan must have come from our Father. It was a whole being.

Gabe hurried down the stairs to the great room. "Too bad we can't build a fire in this fireplace, it is one big one, roast a whole elk."

Jake rubbed the frost on the window, scanning the yard. "Wonder where they keep their extra vehicles? Like to get on down the road not that you guys aren't entertaining with your half-ass plans. My butt can't take any more of that sled."

"You can't go stealing government property like that," said Paul.

"Are you completely friggin nuts!," exploded Jake. You think breakin' and entering and burning down the U S of A's favorite place isn't a problem!"

"Hey man, we haven't done anything but come through an open window. No burning, no breaking," said Paul. "Maybe won't have to."



"Sure," said Jake, "and the Feds will overlook the bear and elk kill as an accident. Who knows what really happened to that sled head. Maybe you meant to kill him."

Paul looked out of the corner of his eye to see how Gabe was taking all this. Gabe's eyes were black and his jaw set as he crossed the room toward Jake.

Grabbing him by the neck and twisting his arm behind him, Gabe drug Jake around looking for a door or any hole to throw him out. They were all boarded up from the outside. Shoving Jake toward the stairs, Gabe yelled, "Get your hide outa here. I'm through putting up with your bullshit." Jake beat his feet up the stairs and down the fire escape.

Gabe looked at Paul. "We are going to have to figure out a way to get warm without the smoke signaling everybody. Not until we are ready, anyway," he added softly. "Light the propane stove to make coffee and cook, but that won't make a dent in this cold. Let's get our gear, sleeping bags and hide the snow machines."

"I still say we pull them in here," said Paul. "Just to be safe."

All of a sudden the same thought occurred to them. "That miserable Jake will run off with 'em," yelled Gabe. "Let's go."

Jake saw them coming just as the snow machine caught. For a moment, he gunned the engine, then slowing it to an idle, he braced himself for their rage.

Reaching him first, Gabe grabbed him by the arm and started

to jerk him off the seat. Suddenly he let go and stepping back, said, "Go, get to gettin', you are a worthless hunk of dog shit and we don't need ya."

"I've been trying to tell you that but you guys just couldn't get enough of me. Let me go and I'll carry a message, talk about your plan. Otherwise, you are sittin here freezing your asses off and nobody will know or give a rip."

"What story are you going to tell?" said Gabe. "And who are you gonna tell?"

"You tell me," said Jake. "I got the notion. You're planning on setting up permanent camp here in Yellowstone to teach folks how to be Indians again. Or steal all the buffalo and take 'em home. I gotta say, it seems pretty lame to me, knowing

that most don't give a rat's ass. Only old people talk about the past. I'm getting off the rez just as soon as I get some cash and I sure as hell ain't livin' here like a primitive."

"Here's the deal Jake. Gabe and I will write something up for you to take to Old Man. For that, you get to take the snow machine and high tail it outa here."

"Don't deliver and you will have two very pissed off Blackfeet hunting you and we'll stretch more than your hide," growled Gabe. "Get inside, first we gotta get some way to get warm."

The sun slid behind the lodge dropping the temperature several degrees.

Reluctantly Jake climbed off the ski-doo and headed back to the lodge with Gabe and Paul. He wondered what had kept him from gunning the sled and making tracks away. Maybe it was the gun Gabe had, but he knew that wasn't it. Gabe wouldn't shoot him. Maybe he just wanted to see how Paul saw it. The dream. Maybe he just wanted to see how far these crazy bastards would go before it got shut down. Jake shook his head, maybe he was plumb crazy too.

Rummaging through the storeroom off the main kitchen they found no can goods left to freeze and burst, only bags of flour, beans and cereals. The big freezers were empty, the electricity shut off. Clearly, Old Faithful was not expecting winter guests.

"We stay in here, we freeze. We can't start a fire, someone will see it, said Gabe. "Outside, it will just look like another steam vent."

"Hey man, I thought that was part of the big dream, burn this joint down," said Jake.

"At the right time, only at the right time," said Paul.

Hunched in their sleeping bags in the shelter of the lodge's wide veranda, they heard Old Faithful spew again. "About every hour and some," said Gabe looking at his watch. "Sure is faithful."

"Do you think the geyser only goes off if there is someone to see it? Kinda like that story about the tree falling in the woods, will it make a sound?" Hearing only a grunt for an answer, Jake pulled the bag over his head and shut his eyes. Leaving tomorrow, no matter what.

##

Old Man reread the letter from Paul and Gabe then pushed

 it across the table to Louie Looking Horse. The tribal council leader's attorney snorted as he scanned the pages.

"Man, oh man, what are these guys smoking? Burn down Old Faithful. Move the Blackfeet Reservation to Yellowstone Park! What's wrong with Glacier Park, at least the tribe's got a legitimate boundary claim there and it's a hell of lot closer. As our chief, Earl Old Person tells it, 'We only sold them the rocks.' We own the rest.'"

"Read it again," instructed Old Man. "They aren't just talking about Yellowstone, but all national parks going back to their original dwellers; Native People – the Crow, Cheyenne, our people the Blackfeet and the Nez Perce and Shoshone."

"Yellowstone is where for long time many tribes came for ceremony and to find warmth in the hotpots and to hunt during the long winter. For a long time now, Indian people cannot hunt in the Parks and for a while not even go there. Yellowstone is today," he said rising to his feet and touching his heart with his hand, "where they make their stand and we must stand with them."

"Yellowstone is where they could die," said Looking Horse tipping back his chair, his head shaking. "They so much as light a cigarette and the Feds will be on them. And there's that possible manslaughter charge hanging out there."

Old Man sat back down and crossed his arms over his chest, his eyes slits in a landscape face of many valleys. "What would you have them do? They are innocent of crime, yet they are hunted."

"They need to come forward. There is support for their case.

They did bring the injured man to the hospital. Course, as Jake tells it, there's the grizzly bear and the elk killing, a federal matter, but, probably understandable under the circumstances. What won't work is holding Old Faithful hostage."

"Remember," said Old Man, "I speak to you with trust. Only you know where they are."

"Don't bet on it grandfather. With Jake loose, it's just a matter of days, maybe hours, before the gig is up. And there are a lot of folks looking for these guys," said Looking Horse.

"Then we waste time here, we go now to Yellowstone. They will need us."

"I'm not good with a fire extinguisher," said Looking Horse, "I put out fires by understanding the law, by being smarter than my opponent and only going at it when there is a chance of winning. This scheme is a losing proposition.

"There is another reason why this theory won't hold rain." said Looking Horse trying to penetrate Old Man's fervor. "Park lands, like reservation lands were initially chosen because the white man could see no commercial value to them. Crops wouldn't grow, only certain animals survive the harshness. Sure, the idea of 'preserving America's natural monuments' played heavier into it later, but you can bet, if the early squatters to our land could have cut a bushel of wheat – landscape monuments, natural grandeur – be dammed, it would have been turned into homesteads.

"It is not feasible to locate a tribe in Yellowstone unless they've got a mail box for their support checks. Even the buffalo are leaving the Park to find food. How long until our people run out of game – kill all the buffalo and the elk and even the rabbits. You'd be trading reservation blues for park rations within six months. It would be no different. The era of living off the land is over."

"This isn't about your learning, this is about your heart, your people's past and more about their future," said Old Man.

"Will you try to talk them into giving this up and letting me help them in the only way that I can?" said Looking Horse.

"I thought you had fire in your belly, but you are bound by books with laws that don't have meaning when it concerns spirit." Old Man's words were spoken just above a whisper, but pierced the distance between them. "You stay here. I go now."

## CHAPTER 16

# HIDE AND SEEK

Agent razor-face evidently did not require sleep. Nor food. Just coffee. It was now almost noon and even his suit had retained its sharp creases.

Red trussed to the kitchen chair strained while every muscle in his body throbbed. His eyelids scraped like sandpaper when he tried to focus on staying awake. Screw the FBI, he had rights and he wasn't about to give this asshole the satisfaction of spilling the whereabouts of Gabe and Paul. He wanted his payback in his own way first.

"Here is your situation," said the agent, his lips curling in a smirk. "You are suspected of aiding and abetting criminals. While we wait for agent Murphy to arrive to transport you to jail, you could make your life a whole lot easier if you come out with where Dumont and Heavy Shield are hiding. If you continue to protect them, I can only assume, despite your protests to the contrary, that you are a major part of the whole affair and will be dealt with accordingly. In other words," the agent put the tip of his loafer on the bottom rung of Red's chair and gave it a shove tipping it over with a crash, "your red ass is about to get nailed."

##

Feral loaded the heavy boxes in the back of the pickup alongside the snow machine and whistled for Cisco. She and that mangy mongrel had forged an understanding. As soon as Gabe was back in the picture that would be over, just like my intentions to stay the hell out of this, she thought ruefully. I hope neighbor Sam never finds out that the truck he loaned me I'm about to give to a couple of dumb, hard-luck Indians, who, if they don't get out, they won't ever be able to. "The thing that's going to be tough for me, Cisco, is explaining that I had yet another vehicle stolen. Hopefully I wouldn't get the same cop." The last one was all manly concern for her being all alone and vulnerable to the very vile men she had given shelter to. The ones who then took advantage of her, stealing her SUV, snow machines, equipment and all. He had strongly cautioned her about showing kindness to strangers, implying that next time, it may not just be her transportation equipment that would be in danger. Clearly she needed a fresh one to work her wiles on.

Parking the pickup in a pullout as the sun set behind the

ridge, she hurriedly unloaded the snow machine and the food. Heading down the trail, the steady hum of the machine lulled her thoughts while it skimmed the tops of the windblown snow. So beautiful, mystical, she thought, is this land with snow circling boiling cauldrons – fire and ice. Is this the story of our universe, she pondered? Opposites creating a tension suspending union. If joined, would one extinguish the other? Doused, as it were? Is that what had happened in her own life? Had she been like the ice putting out the flame of each man who wanted a union with her, dousing their cock-sure belief that they had something she needed. Where was the man who could stoke a fire, a circle of warmth, without turning cold for her greater want. "So Cisco, I am flat out of metaphors about fire, ice, kindling and you sitting back there laughing at me. Careful, I'll turn you into puppy patties, grill you on the deck of Old Faithful and feed you to Gabe."

Feral hoped that Gabe would see Cisco before he shot her. With darkness settling, she was unrecognizable wearing her helmet and snow suit. Approaching the lodge, she wound down the speed and cut to off in front of the massive doors. Cisco jumped off the back like a shot and whipped around the corner barking. He could smell his buddy even before Gabe saw him.

"I've brought brownies and a pickup," she grinned as Gabe looked up at her while he knelt in the snow hugging the frenetic dog. "Course you don't get the brownies if you don't take the truck and get out of here."

"Feral, you've been throwing me out or trying to push me out of about everywhere I land. You are just like the rest of you pale faces."

"That's cause you are so lame at being an Indian, I am frankly embarrassed. You don't know how and where to hide and now, when you could use the traffic, nobody knows where you are. I say we all ride back to where I parked the pickup and you drop me at the ranch and keep going."

"To where? To jail is where I'd end up. We need to stay here and get the government to listen to us," Gabe said as he stood and brushed the snow from his pants. "It's too dark for you to go back tonight, but tomorrow you are long gone."

"Sure I am," smirked Feral.

The three of them crowded in a two-person tent and hurriedly ate the spaghetti and meatballs Feral had brought. It is much easier to do battle on a full stomach.

"By now, Old Man has read the letter we sent and is probably rounding up our people to come here and stand with us," said Paul.

Gabe nodded. Getting a bunch to come up here would be easy. They love to go anywhere, caravan with their friends and family, especially any place where they could get their travel and meals paid for. Old Man would probably promise that. What he couldn't promise is that any of them would stay. Stay and stand together for a better life. While not all, for the people Paul wanted to help, many of their thoughts were about today's misery or tonight's beer, not tomorrow, not the future.

They saw their past as so many words. They had not witnessed the deeds, or lived the bravery for themselves, so they lost the images to show them the way. What made them different than any other forgotten people in America. What made them Indian now.

Their reality was etched bitter cold with the wind blowing disposable diapers out of the reservation town dump and into the trees. Folks called them diaper trees. Horses turned out to find forage when their owners had no cash to buy feed often ate the diapers and died when the plastic wadded up and blocked their intestines.

Almost 200 years had gone since the Indians had discovered Lewis and Clark cutting through their back yard. Within 60 years of that discovery, many native people died from white man's diseases. Some bands lost ninety percent of their tribe from smallpox or were run to ground and forced onto the reservations. They couldn't hunt, hold ceremonies, couldn't survive. It had been a long time since they had chosen their own way of life. Five generations had lived on the reservations. Some prospered in spite of the system, still, Gabe swallowed hard to believe that the lost people, the ones Paul wanted to help, could choose a different path. "Tell me again about the vision," said Gabe.

"Here is how I saw it in my dream," said Paul. "We were in this building there." The small tent held their heat. Outside the night was black, the moon hiding.

"You mean Old Faithful, that one there," Feral said pointing her thumb over her shoulder. “America’s favorite – a testimony of man’s ability to build and dominate said wilderness,” Feral said smirking.

Paul glanced at her, shrugged his shoulder and continued. “There were hundreds of people gathered and the National Guard or the army, a bunch of guys anyway with their guns stood facing the crowd. But no one shot. There were several of us inside and we all had torches and matches and gasoline, but no fire was started.”

“So, said Gabe, “if no one shot and we didn’t torch the joint, what did we do? What happened?”

Paul lowered his voice to a whisper. “I don’t know. Nothing else happened. It faded away, but I know we are to come here.”

Gabe stared at him, the light from the propane stove following the curve of his surprise. Feral started to speak, but with a look at Gabe’s face, swallowed her words.

“Paul, when you said you had a vision, a dream. I didn’t imagine that it was just the previews,” said Gabe.

“Okay, we’ve been here, what two nights,” said Paul, “I need more time, more sleep. There is a fog around me that I can’t see beyond.”

Gabe studied him, saw the fatigue, saw the confusion. “We talk tomorrow.”

Feral pulled her sleeping bag as close as she could to Gabe’s. Still, she ended up in the middle of the small tent between the two men until Cisco came in and pushed his way between her and Gabe’s bag. He lay there panting road kill breath, daring her to try and move him. Gabe rolled over and within seconds was sound asleep.

She could hear Paul sighing and trying to get comfortable. Her butt was pushing against his until he rolled over and flung his arm over her. She wasn't sure what to do. Her fever was for Gabe, Paul struck her as kind of a sissy-ass, all about sacred this and that. If she was going to go native, she planned on climbing on the best of the breed. She held herself tight, waiting for Paul to speak or move closer. He did neither.

Gabe awoke to the sound of a muffled voice coming nearer the tent. In a flash he was up and pointing his rifle at the tent flap ready to blast anyone who came through that door. The faint light meant it was about eight.

The voice fell silent followed by the yipping of what sounded like a rabid coyote. Then another, soon another. Gabe burst through the opening of the tent laughing. "Old Man, you are great hunter and make great coyote." Old Man snow-shoed up close. In the distance, a figure came slowly toward them, falling, getting up, falling again.

Old Man snickered. "We teach Looking Horse how to travel in snow. He not so smart out here. He learn skis pretty quick now. I wondered why you here, Paul, we thought you'd go to where Grandfather Heavy Shield and I always took you. The caves make good hiding."

"We were there," Gabe interrupted, "but things got a little out of hand, we broke a few federal laws by killing a bear and Red killed an elk. But the topper was the park cop jerked loose the innards of our pickup. They were coming in helicopters. Figured it was time to change, to move up."

"Who are you," said Feral.

Old Man looked pointedly from Gabe to Paul and back to Feral. Feral laughed and said, "I don't belong with either one and they didn't kidnap me. I'm here because this is the most idiotic, sadly funny situation I've ever seen and I can't wait for the next scene."

"Old Man," said Paul, "did you talk to our people? When are they coming?"

"Not sure," replied Old Man.

"I bet they never come," said Feral. "The old ones don't want to leave their comfortable beds, the young don't want to

leave television. Maybe you should wait for summer. This real estate might look friendly then."

Paul felt his face burn. Except for the fact that she always brought good food, she reminded him of the wolverine. He wished he had a hatchet he'd bring it down square on her big mouth.

"Times are different, the people are different," agreed Gabe wearily, "the young guys are punks, they wear white man's basketball numbers on their chest, not the sacred drawings of our times."

"The land will cleanse their spirits," murmured Old Man.

"This land could bury them," retorted Gabe.

Paul stared at Gabe in disbelief. "I thought you could see with me. You seemed to be, now you've turned your back."

##

"That Billy the Sioux is out on bail," Lucy whispered to Red. "He's got lots to say about the meat heist and you. He is blaming you for the whole thing."

Red keeping his eye always on the FBI agent, cursed.

"What are you two talking about," demanded razor face. Before they had a chance to reply, the agent's cell phone rang. After a long conversation peppered black with bureaucratic jargon, the FBI agent informed them he had been called back to Butte and couldn't wait for his replacement. "I am going to demand that the tribal police hold you both in house arrest until further notice. "You," he said pointing at Lucy, "for harboring a criminal."

Red paced the small house, torn between finding Gabe and Paul, especially that asshole Gabe, or turning them in. Playing games with the FBI was a drag, especially tied to a kitchen chair. At least now he could move around. He had friends in the tribal police force. House arrest was a joke. "Red leaves when he's ready." He'd get his strength back in a day or two. He'd leave after he'd slept as long as he could and had his way with Lucy as many times as he was able. Then he'd go find them boys and let them know that he hadn't ratted them out cause he was saving them for himself.

##

With the arrival of Looking Horse looking like winter kill, after he took his skis off and tried to wade through two feet of snow for the last quarter mile, they made plans for the coming days. Old Man had brought lots of provisions so they could feed the people and also five tents. Most of the stuff was still in the van parked about two miles away. They had left the vehicle at a graded pull-out where skiers started their trek into the back country of Yellowstone, figuring they would blend in. Better than trying to hide the van or parking it in some remote place where it would arouse suspicion. They could run the snow machines to pick up supplies. But first, they needed a headquarters. Sleeping outside was not for aging warriors.

"I see you can get in the building," said Old Man. "Why do you sleep outside?"

"There is no way to heat the joint and it is really, really big and freezing ass cold," said Gabe.

"Why don't you use generator," said Old Man. "All important buildings have generators. Look around."

Sure enough, down in the basement which held the heat plant was a generator that ran on gasoline. Gabe, Paul, Looking Horse and Feral stood there staring at it as if waiting for it to speak. Clearly, they were clueless as to how it operated.

"Go to motor vehicle shop down there and get gasoline," said Old Man. "I have to tell you everything."

"Woman, find electric panel, switch only kitchen on."

"With all due respect, Mr. Old Man," said Feral, "I don't take to being ordered around without a please in front of it."

Old Man scrutinized Feral as if seeing her for the first time. "White woman, switch on kitchen. I thank you." A faint smile crinkled his eyes. "Words, words, so important to you people."

"Why just the kitchen?" said Feral. "Why not the whole place?"

"Too big. Too cold," said Old Man. "Close the doors, heat the kitchen and open those big ovens, warm things up right quick."

"Are we going to sleep in the kitchen," said Feral, "what about taking a pee?"

"Hang it out the window," Gabe quipped.

All day they traveled back and forth between the van and lodge hauling supplies. And waited and watched for their people to come. Swigging tea after a supper of ham and beans, they turned their attention to Paul. He talked more of his recent ideas that the tribes could take over the national parks all over the country. He'd been thinking that maybe just trying to live off the land might not work long-term. They could operate the lodges, scalp the tourists themselves. We are due this, long overdue. The parks aren't getting the money. It goes to Washington.

Gabe agreed, but he wanted only the buffalo to take back to the reservations.

"So, your plans to burn down Old Faithful seem even more stupid than before," said Feral. "Since you are planning on becoming the landlord, have your peoples play the role of noble savage," she said.

"We may have to," Paul said. "We need something to bargain with."

"It's one crazy thing to demand the land, even the buffalo," argued Feral, "but all the buildings, the infrastructure, no way in hell will they give that investment up. Somebody somewhere is getting rich off this."

"Our land was rich with what we needed before the white man came," said Paul. "They used it all up, stripped Mother Earth of grass, trees, buffalo, even the bear. Times have changed, I know that. But the lumber for these buildings, this lodge came from the earth here. These places belong to the earth. We belong to the earth. If we are to live our culture, we must create the right environment. Live in the natural order of the earth."

"Ergo, you and the lodge are in it together, relations as it were," said Feral wryly.

"You just love to hear yourself talk, don't you," said Gabe pointing at Feral. She started to reply but Gabe put his hand over her mouth, none too gently.

Paul ignored them. "Now they say we must protect wolves and grizzly. They call them endangered species. We are the endangered species. Indian people are barely surviving on the reservations. We'll swap the reservations for this."

Looking Horse had sat back from the others. He knew they were not ready to talk sense. Finally, he could hold his words no longer.

"Why, why would they do that," he demanded. "You people need to think about your situation. You are in no position to bargain. Your logic is that of a child." Slamming out the door, he threw over his shoulder, "When you are ready to face reality we can talk." That night he slept in the tent alone.

##

Old Man heard the machine come over the ridge first. Gabe and Paul had gone down to the shed to check out how much fuel was available for the generator. Feral was at her chosen hotpot where the ground was clear of snow and she could squat across a log in privacy. The lights were off in the kitchen, the place looked deserted except for the small tent and one snow mobile. A man and woman climbed off their snow machine carrying TV camera gear.

Old Man stood by the tent as the news crew drug their equipment up the slope. He hoped Paul and Gabe would stay hidden.

"Sir, I am Kate Moore a reporter from KFQF out of Great Falls and this is my camera guy, Phil. Who are you?" Before he could answer, she rushed on. "We got a tip that Paul Heavy Shield and Gabe Dumont are here hiding and planning something big." She thrust the mike in his face.

"I come here in winter to pray, take the water in. I look for no one. I have only small tent, the lodge is boarded up, where would they be?" Just then Cisco ran toward them barking. Old Man grabbed his collar as he went for the camera guy. "I bring my dog."

Kate Moore looked around and back at Old Man. "So you haven't seen anyone."

"Sure, lots of people on snow machines come by, but they

don’t stop, they must be in a hurry. I come here to seek solace, not looking for company.”

“Do you know Heavy Shield and Dumont? They are the ones who were involved in the injury of that Ohio man.”

“I know them, since they were little boys. They are good men. They work hard to serve their people.”

Rounding the corner with a roll of toilet paper in hand, Feral stopped short. Phil caught a glimpse of her and started to run in that direction, the camera perched on his shoulder. Feral didn’t know which way to go. Head into the side door and expose their living quarters, down to the machine shop and blow the cover. I need a story quick she thought.

Turning around, she pushed past camera guy and headed toward Old Man. Looking at her through veiled eyes, he said, “Sometimes I bring my friend.”

Kate Moore looked from Old Man to Feral to Cisco. “Who else can we expect at this solo prayer retreat?”

Feral looked at Old Man and grinned and wondered where Louie Looking Horse was. He had joined them for breakfast after spending the night in the tent sulking because they wouldn’t listen to him. He informed them that they would need him soon enough.

The reporter turned her attention to Feral asking her who she was, what she was doing there and if she had seen the two men. Feral thought for a moment and told her that she was looking for any trace of her stolen vehicles. She had borrowed her neighbor’s truck and the snow machine that was parked there to scout around as the men who had taken her SUV had mentioned seeing Yellowstone in the winter. Though at the time she had thought they were joking. Old Man had offered her a cup of coffee and they had visited and she planned to head home after checking the area.

"If that's her snow machine, how did you get here," Phil's eyes narrowed in suspicion.

"No worries," said Old Man, "nephew come for me end of week."

Kate seemed about to question this last statement, but looking from one to the other, realized they were both too cagy for her. Besides, maybe they were just two crazies out on their own adventure and she had a bigger story to tell.

"We are going to be staying over at the Snow Lodge, where it is warm and there is food, but we will be back often to see if anyone else has shown up. Would you come get me if they show? The publicity will help them. They can tell their side of the story."

Old Man and Feral assured her they would and waved as they drove away.

"Oh yeah," said Feral, "I will be hot footing it right over."

Shaking his head Old Man scolded her for her lack of savvy. "News coverage come in handy to bring the world to this door, to help tell our story. Just need plan first. Make after lunch."

Spreading the mayonnaise over the thick slices of bread and venison, Feral heard the sound of knocking at the big doors. The guys were out gathering wood for the small wood stove used in the kitchen for burning trash. Fuel for the generator would run out in a couple of days and require either a trip to town for more or bring an end to their winter carnival. Staying in the shadows, she made her way through the frigid great room to look out a side window. There were maybe 15 people on snowshoes standing in the yard. "Just figures," she murmured, "make a sandwich and the whole damn world wants to eat. I have got to get out of here. Much longer and my bullshit story of rounding up vehicle rustlers won't spin."

His arms full of wood, Looking Horse surveyed the crowd gathered in front of the lodge. He had only come because Old Man had asked him. It was craziness and he had half a mind to drop the wood right there and head down the trail. This hope that putting people who lived in houses, not tipis for generations, in the wilderness would make real Indians out of them was crazy. He had left the rez many years ago and got an education. He was equal to any lawyer in Billings. He had no dreams.

## CHAPTER 17

# BY SLED, TRAVOIS AND PROMISES

Old Man hurried toward the people. Children were strapped on the backs of their parents and one old couple rode on a travois pulled by two men. As they came closer to the lodge their steps slowed, their gaze tentative. Paul and Gabe arrived and climbed up on the wide porch to welcome them. Paul's confidence rose as the group moved closer to hear him. Gabe wondered what they were going to do now. What did these people expect, what had they been promised? Would they feel what Paul saw?

The wood they had gathered was stacked in the yard and the snow pushed away. A fire would pull the people together. Old Man sat off to one side and unfolded a buffalo robe on the packed snow. Reaching inside he withdrew three bundles wrapped in buckskin tied with leather thongs. Untying the sinew, he carefully laid out a smudge stick of sage and pine needles, a braid of sweet grass, an eagle feather, buffalo horn, a sacred bone whistle and a small drum. The last bundle lay before him in front of the fire.

Forming a cross-legged circle, the people begin to chant low pacing to the Old Man's rhythmic lead. Purifying himself by waving the smoke from the smudge over his face and chest, he invited each to do so in turn. Then unwrapping the final bundle, Old Man lit then offered the pipe to the four directions. The smoke curled around the bowl lifting their prayers to the heavens. Passing the pipe to Paul, he said in Pikani – Blackfeet, "We welcome the people to honor the vision – to see a tomorrow filled with the pride of our people." The pipe made the circle and drew them closer to the flame, the vision, as Paul spoke of his dream.

More began to arrive. They came on snowmobiles, snowshoes and pulled sleds with children and old ones. Many were Crow and Cheyenne as their reservations were closest to the Park. Few came prepared to spend the night in the cold. All were hungry from the two-mile trek from the road.

Gabe had the big ovens in the kitchen roasting elk meat and potatoes. Feral was sent to the only open gas station in the Park as the generators were drinking fast. Filling the cans, she told the attendant that her power was out at the ranch and she was running off a generator. She pulled the load behind her snow mobile on a sled and pondered whether to dump the load at the lodge and head for home or stay. But she knew she wouldn't leave. When would she ever get an experience like this again.

As the afternoon faded into twilight, the cold settled in. Tonight they could squeeze those who did not have camping gear into the kitchen, but not tomorrow as the crowd grew. The food would last for maybe three or four days depending on how many more came.

Paul had spent the day moving through the people sharing his dream, asking for their counsel. It was hard to answer how they could live out here when even the buffalo left the Park in search of food. Paul felt the cold as some stopped talking as he approached and huddled together as he moved on. He wondered if Feral was right, maybe a summer showdown would have worked better. He felt the reason, but not the way.

Gabe listened to the radio anxious for the news report. From the announcer's update, he knew the park rangers had found the cave and the not so happy hunting ground. The injured snow machine driver was upgraded from critical. For a moment he felt like going to Paul and asking him to call it all off. But Paul needed this chance to see the reality – not the vision. He would only accept the truth coming from his people. He might listen as they tell him that living off the land – it's a century too late. Maybe then he would see the logic of bringing the buffalo home to the rez.

Just as he was turning the radio off to save the battery,

Feral's name was mentioned as a possible missing person. Her neighbor had gone over to help her feed cattle and she and his snow machine and truck were gone. Her prior stolen vehicle led to speculation that whoever took it came back for her. Anyone seeing her was urged to call the police. They had been unable to reach her father as of yet.

"I knew you were trouble." Feral turned toward Gabe's firm hand on her arm.

"I thought you liked trouble," she retorted, "what now?"

"Your neighbor turned you in to missing persons. Maybe he was concerned about you or just wants his pickup back, but you are on the news right after our story. The only good thing is the sledder is out of ICU, but I don't think he is sitting up quite yet. But you get out of here. We don't need the local sheriff finding us looking for you."

"Dammit, he's got lots of trucks. I left him a note on my front door but it must have blown off. He lent me that pickup and sled until mine are found. I am sure," she said with a smirk, "Red will bring back my Blazer just any day now. And just so you know," she said pulling her arm away, "I'm not leaving just yet."

As night fell, the bonfire burned brighter. There were no dances, no songs, only quiet talk. Inside the lodge kitchen, the ancient debate of Indian rights volleyed with the concept of what Paul was proposing. They painted stories of the tribes running the lodges, gift shops, grocery stores, acting as guides and dancers and drummers. The women joked they would hire white folks for cleaning and cooking, because with this new plan, they would be rich like those Pequot tribes with their casinos.

Louie Looking Horse listened and twitched. His time would come, he would get them to see. But not tonight, tonight was about the dream. When the food ran out they might listen to reason then. Hope had thinly wrapped despair for most of their lives. They wanted to believe that their past and future were intertwined, that they could move forward by looking back. He was very surprised when he met Paul, who had lived in Seattle and had been away from the rez for years, had succumbed to the Hollywood version of Indian life. Louie was raised in Billings and had gone to law school in Denver. He took a job with the tribes so he could stay in Montana. His dream was today. Learn from the past, from white men. Beat them at their game.

Louie had always heard talk about the "natural order" of Indians and their land. Like Gabe, he couldn't deny what he saw day in day out. Reservation people, isolated from the world by apathy and prejudice, became defined by those pressures. Powwow pride was not enough to give them the grit – the belief in self - needed to battle alcohol, drugs and their own jealousy of each other. From the old stories, some had a vague sense about who they had been, but the history books had been written by the conquering race. Whites ascribed words to create the legacy of the noble savage. Who was creating the story now? Who is the 21st Century Indian? Are they stuck in that place between what was and what is and what will be?

Paul stayed in a tent that night with other men. Now that the people had come, the excitement about a glorious future had cooled with the embers of the campfire – the cold, stark landscape. He knew he had no real plan on how to create it. Paul had always thought of himself as a seeker. The idea guy. Working with the kids in Head Start he talked to them about their tomorrow, a world of their own design, regardless of their current home life. But he was reminded that there were tough years ahead each time his kids talked about the police coming to their house.

With torch in hand, what should he demand? And if he succeeded, would his people become the new profit seekers, care-taking for currency. What had he started? Sleep on it, dream on it. Tomorrow it will be seen.

##

Kate Moore heard the rapping on her door, but a glance at the dark window told her it was either very late or too early. She stuffed the pillow over her head. Seconds later she heard it again only louder. Cursing, she wrapped herself in the blanket and opened the door. Old Man was walking down the steps his snowshoes under his arm. Looking back, he waved to her and called out, “Come now, bring TV camera.”

Flipping pancakes was not Feral’s idea of a great adventure, but Gabe had volunteered her. He stood beside her frying bacon and tossing both on plates while hustling the crowd through the kitchen. “I’m thinking this is all wrong. What’s your reason to stay," he poked Feral. 

"Why I am just crazy with the notion," she drawled, "of you people taking over the Park, like you deserve it. But I was counting on Old Faithful burning down. Is there any chance that could still happen? People would remember that for the rest..." her voice trailed off.

Outside, reporter Kate Moore and Phil the camera guy were busy setting up. Feral thought it best that she stayed out of camera range. She figured she'd better go back to the gas station and call her neighbor before the morning was over and tell him she's fine, the snow machine is fine, and that she had offered his truck to the fugitives. Maybe not tell him that.

Paul decided to focus the first interview on the accident. He explained that the buffalo were in danger of suffocating from the ice in their lungs from running in cold. "One of the babies went down right in front of us," he said, "he couldn't keep up, the little one was trampled to death." Trying to explain how the snow machine ended up crashing into a tree with the driver on the ground did sound unreal, he admitted. "Ya had to be there." He ended with a plea. "The buffalo, the wild places, and Indian people are endangered species. We need to be united."

Louie Looking Horse stepped forward, leaning over Paul to speak into the mike. "We will fight this out in court," he said. Paul angrily pushed him back. "We will make our stand here."

The reporter, seeing an interesting headline to the story,

"Indian Faction Split," moved toward Louie with Gabe right behind him, pressing close. "I need to consult with my clients before issuing any information." Louie's eyes were slits in his drawn face. And then he was gone.

Reporter Kate Moore, wanted more. "Why Yellowstone? Why Old Faithful?" But the people turned their backs. The TV crew packed up their gear with a "We will be back." Kate knew she had a great story already. The problem was, if she alerted the public to the whereabouts of Dumont and Heavy Shield, they would be arrested and the story would be much shorter and a whole lot less exciting. She had some editing to do.

Packing up their equipment, Kate whispered to Phil, "We need to find that guy spouting legal talk. The old man can be our first story, legal guy next. That will give us enough while we see what they are up to next. I want to save Dumont and Heavy Shield as long as I can."

Feral decided it was time to call her neighbor. She started up the snow machine and strapped the gas tanks on the back. Gabe spotted her. "Ready to go home?"

"I'm planning to do you a great big favor. I'm getting more gasoline and I'm calling my neighbor to tell him that I am not being held hostage and ravished by a savage, unless of course you'd like to do that, the call can wait."

"I'm thinking you oughta tell him in person."

"And miss yet another catastrophe – work in progress – currently known as the 'dream.'"

Gabe moved closer. Pulling her to him, he tilted her head back, his hand tangled in her hair. Kissing her hard, he picked her up and set her on the snow machine, revved the engine and pointed down the trail. "Now, bitch, get."

The pale sun was sitting on the horizon as she sited Old Faithful. The conversation with her neighbor had gone down poorly. Once the initial relief was over, he accused her of being reckless. She told him she was holed up with an old trapper with no phone, but would start her way back to the ranch tomorrow or the next day. She hung up as his voice got louder. Bad connection.

She could see that many more had come in the space of the three hours since she left. She was surprised at their willingness to trek in from the highway. It had to be to two miles of thigh-high snow pack.

From a distance it had the look of a painting from the 1800s. A slight wind lifted the snow creating a white gauze shroud across the scene. A drum beat out a slow heartbeat rhythm. People milled around the fire, smoke soft shaping their features, their garments.

Suddenly the wind shifted and the contrast of man and fire and snow was stark. Flames pierced the air, her breath caught in her throat. Feral felt a sorrow consume her for all things lost; these people, herself. Adrift, forgotten. The world had changed even in her lifetime. You can't go back she wanted to scream to them but knew they would not hear.

Heading through the side door, she heard Gabe and Paul

arguing. She stepped inside the mud room off the kitchen to listen.

"Paul, you are an idealist." Gabe's voice was low and measured. "You live in a world of dreams. I know this country, it is harsh and survival goes to the ones who know it. It is not for a people who live in town and buy their meat packaged. Those who have learned to make their own way won't come here to live off the land. See that lineup for chili," he pointed toward the kitchen where Old Man was dishing up food. "That will be our story. Can we talk about reality for a minute? What do you really want out of this? And is this about you, not them at all."

Louie Looking Horse stood off to the side, a slight smile touched his lips.

CHAPTER 18

# I GOTTA BEAD ON YA

Red eyed his jailer. Just his luck that they would send a rookie, not a buddy, or even a guy who owed him a favor. The TV blared the story of the missing Dumont and Heavy Shield and a new twist; Kenny had surfaced. A trucker had called in when he found Kenny in the back of the pickup at a quick stop, no driver in sight. Kenny's foot had to be amputated and the story he told led officials back into the park to search for his "kidnappers." He cursed them all and Red was at the top of his list. Now there was no getting out of it, Red thought. Kenny had him cast as the chief troublemaker – the major bad ass. Red gripped Lucy hard, his frustration boiling. "You distract that prick sitting in our kitchen cause

Red's goin' to find those boys and kick their asses good. Since I'm branded as part of their stupid shenanigan, I'm gonna get mine." The dinner Lucy fed the deputy had a hardy dose of sleeping pills. The phone was ripped from the wall.

Late that night when the deputy was zonked, they slipped out with his keys and cell phone. Grinding away with the battery putting out less and less juice, Red had an idea. The truck was identified by now. Probably that bitch Feral told them her cooked up story about being a good Samaritan only to have her vehicle stolen by asshole Red. No worries, he would teach her good. Meanwhile, he could borrow the deputy's truck and it would be several hours before anyone would find it. Who would stop a tribal police vehicle? Lucy said she was going with him. "No matter where I try to hide they will find me. This not knowing what is going to happen to you, to Gabe and Paul is killing me."

Red caught the last name and threw it back at her. "Paul, so this is about Paul, that lying bastard. Red apple dude comes back from the city to tell us how to be. He's here to get you back, Lucy. No shittin' me."

Lucy stared straight ahead, her cheeks burning. "He left me and now I am with you."

##

That night, the people huddled closer around the fire, too many now to spread their blankets in the kitchen. The great room of Old Faithful was colder than the outside. Tents huddled down in the brush like the wild beings around them provided some shelter. As the embers died, the wail of a baby vibrated through the darkness. By midnight, fifty people lined up at the front door of Old Faithful Inn. They were carrying a downed tree and limbs. "Open the door, let us in, we are here to claim our heritage, we've been out in the cold too long."

Drinking tea in the kitchen Feral nudged Paul and laughed, "They've got a point. Seems silly to worry about smoke coming out of the chimney when what you want is to get noticed."

The flames roared in the immense fireplace, a four-story rock structure with an open hearth on all four sides centered on the main floor. Standing as close as they dared, the people rotated from the outer circle in, while the warmth attempted to penetrate the cold.

Each floor of the Inn was held up by tree columns, with sturdy branch arms. Their warm wood color belied the chill. Climbing to the second and third floors, the people found the sleeping rooms, but the heat would not reach them. They pulled the mattresses off the beds and threw them over the balcony around the fireplace. The fire roared and slowly the cold moved out from the circle of beds. The camp had grown to over 75 people from four tribes.

##

Jake tapped his foot nervously. Brother Billy was standing before the judge waiting for his get-out-of-jail card. Breaking into the game station was one thing, but Billy was going to have to go to trial for trying to sandwich that deputy in the trunk of his own police car. Posting bond had been real tough for Jake. Funny how close family become distant cousins when money is needed.

Walking out of the courtroom, Billy grumbled, "I got 30 days to find that bastard Red and teach him what the Sioux Nation do with traitors. He left me behind to get caught. I walked out that door and he was long gone. Next thing, I gotta a 357 barrel shoved up my nose. Yup, I'm gonna fix him good."

"Last time I laid eyes on Red, he took off with some gal's Bronco. She was some hot-headed woman that Gabe met up with in Yellowstone. We was staying at her ranch after shootin' the griz and dumping him out of the pickup. I had to haul Kenny into town – he cooked his foot in a hotpot."

Billy turned and looked at him. "What are you jawin 'about? What bear, what ranch? You shoulda hightailed it home right away. You ain't got no sense."

"You just hadda be there," said Jake.

"Get in, we're goin to catch me a yellow dog."

##

"I'm thinking they made it to the lodge by now," said Red. He and Lucy had driven all night and found a restaurant hooked to a rundown motel. Food and sleep in that order announced Red. "We need our go-getum and ole Red's gone." Lucy ran hot water in the rust-stained tub. Not enough, but some comfort. Lying there while the water cooled in the drafty bathroom, she thought about Paul. Red's anger would sit on Gabe, but she knew he was jealous of Paul. Thought she still cared. Who would she stand beside? Sliding deeper in the tub, she cringed at the knowing.

It was late afternoon when they woke and decided that they would get snowshoes and food and head out in the early morning. They had left Browning rather hurriedly. Drinking beer in the bar that night, they watched the news, but the Jew's attack on the Gaza Strip was the only story. Local interest was focused on stories about old people and how they lived so long. "Gabe's mug won't make that show," Red said.

##

Paul stood on the second floor overlooking the scene below. He knew he had to give his people some sense to the gathering. A reason to stay. The smell of wet wool, smoke and unwashed bodies wafted up to him. It reminded him of wet dog, maybe bear breath; his own shirt after five days with no shower.

"We gonna set up our rez here," yelled a guy sacked out on a mattress. His cigarette smoke clouded his face.

"Done with the rez. Come summer we gonna live here, sleep upstairs, have white folks bring room service, tote our suitcases. We the landlords now."

"If the buffalo gotta leave to eat, we do too," replied another. "I wanna go home. Take the buffalo with me."

Louie Looking Horse stood in the middle of the room. Pointing up at Paul, he shouted, "Well dream boy, what are we going to eat here? What about medical care and education?"

Paul tightened. "My people, what do you want for your life?" For a moment there was silence, then.

"Money!" The voice rang out clear and strong.

"Yea, yea," the crowd laughed and chanted, "money, money. Lots a money."

From the back of the room, a man stood up with a rifle aimed at the balcony. It was impossible to tell if he was pointing at Paul or at Gabe. A woman close to the man screamed and grabbed at the gun. He slapped her back. The people scattered.

"Ole Red don't much care which one of ya I shoot first."

"Hold your fire ole Red, cause I got a bead on you, yellow dog," Billy stepped out from behind one of the massive columns with his rifle pointed at Red's back.

Just then, the television crew with Old Man in the lead burst through the front door. "Paul, Paul, come quick, tell vision. Park rangers on the way."

Paul and Gabe stared down at the scene. This is not at all what they expected. Seeing Old Man leading the TV crew through the crowd looking for Paul, while Billy sited his shotgun on Red, Gabe laughed until tears ran down his face. "You know, Feral's got a point, we are screw ups. I say we head down that fire escape."

"I can't just run out, I am responsible for these people," said Paul.

"No you aren't," Gabe said. "They are leaving. You are responsible for filling their heads with a half-baked idea, but they got a couple of meals. Old Man will give them gas money. A week from now it will just be a story. Might even come up again in the spring. And, what do you bet Feral's got some kinda vehicle parked outside."



"She never does seem to run out," grinned Paul.

Reaching the ground, the two men ran around the front of the building and spotted a 4-wheel drive Browning police truck. Jerking open the cab door, Gabe saw the keys in the ignition. Throwing the stuff on the seat in the back, Gabe realized that this was the vehicle that Red drove in. Now Paul started to howl with laughter. Could it get any better!

"Ya know," grinned Gabe, "we coulda taken a rig that didn't have a wanted poster on the door. That crazy-ass Red. Stealing a cop rig from the tribe, that's ballsy."

Backing it in reverse, Gabe eased out of the yard, keeping his eyes on the front door of the lodge. "Seeing how we are stealing it from Red, I'd say we'd be the ballsy ones. Or, maybe just so used to shit happening, we just go with it."

"Where we going?" said Paul.

"Beats me," said Gabe. "What the hell, the rez or the cave. They won't expect that. We gotta wait it out till we know what happens to that sled head. He's getting better. We can try to talk our way out of this unless he gets worse. Then, we need a fast horse."

"Or an attorney," said Paul. "Sure, we can always claim it wasn't us doing all this crazy shit. It was dumb ass Red and Billy. Not us."

Watching his rear view mirror Gabe saw Feral come out of the lodge and start to run towards them. He gunned the engine throwing snow and mud and headed down the trail. The snow was pounded down from many feet. "Oh shit, I forgot my dog."

##

Old Man looked down at the floor, "I don't know where anybody go." His voice echoed in the majestic room, the fireplace crackling with dying embers. "Me all alone, but no worries, nephew come pretty quick." The two officers surveyed the room. There were mattresses everywhere along with dirty dishes and clothes.

"You may be alone now, but from the looks of things, you had quite a party here," snarled the officer.

"No party, just vision seekers."

"Well," said the officer, "were two of those vision seekers

Paul Heavy Shield and Gabe Dumont? And what about a guy named Red?"

Just then Feral came through the kitchen door, Cisco following.

"Sometimes friend stops by," said Old Man.

Seeing the officers, Feral turned to leave.

"Stop, I am armed," yelled the policeman.

"Well, if you put it that way," said Feral, coming toward Old Man and the two officers. Cisco kept his distance snarling.

"What is your part in this?"

Feral looked quizzical and then blurted, "I evidently supply getaway rigs and snowmobiles for crazy Indians. Course, it's against my will you understand. I've run out 'em – rigs, I mean. Could I bum a ride back to my ranch from you guys?"

"I got Chevy truck back at pullout," said Old Man brightly.

"No you don't," said the officer. "As we drove in, there was a man and a woman pulling out in a Chevy pickup. At that point we had no reason to stop them."

"I bet it's Red," blurted Feral.

"What do you know about Red? You two are coming with us, we got a lot of questions."

"I'm bringing the dog," said Feral.

"He stays."

"He goes."

##

It was hot in the cab, the heater full blast to keep the frost off the windshield. Gabe yawned loudly. "I don't know what we're doing. I feel like I got one foot nailed down and I'm runnin' in circles. It might be a big mistake to go back to the rez, but we can't just sit here on the side of the road. The pale late afternoon sun was fading, the highway stretched black and forever against the greying snow banks.

"You sure Old Man will get home?" said Paul. "Do we need gas? I want to eat and there's a truck stop with a burger joint up ahead." Pulling into the station, the air was thick from the diesel trucks belching smoke. Paul jabbed at the window. "Isn't that Old Man's pickup, it has Browning plates."

"Sure looks like his. Wonder how he got here before us," said Gabe. "I'll fill up, you get us a table and see what he's planning now." The glass door to the cafe was smudged a dirty yellow-grey from cigarette smoke and boot marks. Paul, anxious to get into the warmth pushed through a couple of truckers headed out.

"Watch it buddy," snarled one. "This joint is goin to the dogs," said the second guy, his stale sweat mixed with onions trailed behind.

Lucy saw him first, her eyes huge, cloaked with fear. Red sat across from her, his back to the door.

Slowly Red turned around just as the door slammed shut again. Paul hit the icy pavement butt first. Gabe finishing up at the pump, looked up, shook his head snickering.

"Get the hell out of here," yelled Paul, scrambling to his feet. He made the last 15 feet skating across the lot.

"What's up, why are you all jumpy?"

"Drive, it's Red."

Jumping in the cab, Gabe saw Red poke his head out of the cafe door. His rifle followed. He aimed and fired. Gabe hit the gas pedal and whipped around the truck in front of him. The same surly driver who'd bumped Paul was just putting the gasoline hose back. He dropped to his knees holding his arm and yelling.

"Oh shit, Red shot that guy!"

"What guy?"

"Some tough guy I bumped into coming out of the cafe. Let him tangle with Red. What's he thinking! Shooting with a bunch of people and gasoline around."

"Red doesn't think, he just blows," said Gabe.

"What's his deal, I know he is pissed, but shooting to kill.

What have I ever done to him and he ended up with my girl," said Paul.

"Maybe he wants to make damn sure she don't go back to you," smirked Gabe. Sliding sideways, Gabe spun the pickup up on the highway, but was headed the wrong way. "Whoa, Napi sending us back," Paul grabbed the dashboard.

"We ain't got time to turn around. Red's coming unless that dude he shot or his buddies stops him." In the yard surrounding the gas pumps and cafe, they saw Red dodging low and dragging Lucy around the trucks in the lot toward Old Man's pickup. A couple of lanes away, two big truckers carrying tire irons were closing in.

"Go back or go forward? I'm for getting our asses outa here."

"Will Lucy be okay? What if one of those guys grabs her or beats her up," said Paul as he scraped the frost from the inside window. "I can't leave her."

"They are not going to hurt her. Red's the one who shot their buddy. We aren't going back. Are we going back?"

Paul's frantic look answered that question.

"Are they gonna know one Indian from another. Too bad Billy isn't here," said Gabe.

Paul jumped from the truck and ducking down made his way behind the two guys searching all the truck cabs. He hoped they wouldn't turn around. He hadn't seen Red or the rig yet.

Just then Old Man's truck with Red slouched behind the wheel squealed around the side of the cafe. Lucy stood in the middle of the road watching the back-end of the pickup fishtailing down the road. Gabe couldn't see where Paul was but it didn't look like Red was waiting for anyone. Pulling up beside Lucy, he shoved opened the door. Paul came running with two guys close behind. Grabbing Lucy, he shoved her in the door and climbed up behind her. Gabe popped the clutch. They spun out and took off barely missing Billy as he swung into the parking lot. Seeing Red roaring down the highway, Billy started after him.

Up the road, they could see a patrol car charge out of the pullout, turn on his light and with the siren screaming, close the distance to Red. Billy pulled over.

"Don't want to go past that cop car and Red, so it's the cave for now." Gabe glanced around Lucy to Paul. "Still hungry?"

##

A grim Looking Horse followed Old Man and Feral out of the police station. For once, Feral was silent.

"Your bail is posted. Go home and stay there till the hearing for breaking and entering," he looked pointedly at Feral. "Old Man, until Paul and Gabe surface, there is nothing more for you or any of us to do. The guy in the hospital doesn't even remember them. He thinks his buddy brought him in, course this is the same buddy who ran over him. Don't see how they can build a case against our guys on that. But they got other troubles – poaching, breaking and entering. I am taking you back to the rez."

"I have no ride. If you see those two or that asshole Red,

remind them they owe me." 

"Take a cab, Feral," said Looking Horse

##

That news interview with Feral makes me think that maybe we should go visit her. I bet she misses us, especially you, stud," said Paul.

"Oh you betcha. She'd welcome us with a shotgun. This cave is really getting old though. And that stinking bear getting ripe, real bad, real soon," said Gabe.

"Worse than this rotten egg smell," said Lucy, "could anything be worse?"

"Ooh yea. Here's the deal. Until that sledder is back on his feet – opps – lost one – back on his foot and we know who he blames, we lie low," said Gabe. "He and Kenny, footless, but between the two, a pair. Okay, not funny."

"Nobody is looking for me, not even Red apparently," said Lucy with a hollow laugh. "Why not drop me close to town. I'm going to hang around the hospital and see what I can find out."

"I suspect Red is in the tank. Shooting a trucker, drugging that deputy, stealing his truck and skipping out on the FBI; I'm thinking he is a goner at least for a while. Course, we have the deputy's truck. But enough about our fun times, you are going to get a chocolate bar, aren't you," added Paul softly. "You never could go longer than a couple of days without...umm, chocolate as I remember."

Lucy looked down a small smile touching her lips.

“Our spray paint job on the truck throws ‘em off and the muddy license plate. We can’t sit here too long though, the Feds are going to decide to check this cave again, or they are dumber than I thought,” said Gabe. “We’ll be at Feral’s. Call this number,” he said, handing her a slip of paper. “If not there, Old Faithful and bring a match. You stay out of sight and outa trouble.”

CHAPTER 19

# BUFFALO PURE

“Chairman,” said Louis Looking Horse, “In 1992, the newly formed Intertribal Bison Cooperative petitioned the Feds to let the tribes run buffalo herds on the reservations. Most have.”

“Those buffalo, they are like ‘half-breed’ - they are buffalo cattle. Just like some of our people who go with whites and dilute the blood,” said the chairman. “The only pure blood lines in the world, the wild ones, are in Yellowstone. Those are the ones we bring into safe keeping. They are the only direct living link to the millions of buffalo that once roamed this country.

“We have prayed on this decision and know it must be done, the time – our time – is now.” said the Blackfeet chair.

"Our warriors dream bigger than our people can do. We can't live in the wilds, in the parks. They are no longer our sacred ground. Yes, the reservations are hard places, but our ancestors are there now. But the buffalo – the wild, free, pure ones – they are our sacred brothers, they can't survive in Yellowstone either. They are shot every time they leave the Park. We will bring them back to the reservations. They will roam as in old days, restore our people, our herds. Give life to the natural order. Then our people will heal."

"The ranchers will fight you," said Looking Horse.

The council nodded in agreement. Shaking his head, the Sioux chair stated, "Ranchers don't care about elk eating their hay. They don't believe that elk carry Brucellosis and give it to

cattle. They blame the buffalo. Since the '90s, there's been over 3,000 pure blood buffalo shot as they left the park in search of food, even though there has never been a documented case of buffalo infecting cattle."

"Our creation story tells us that buffalo were once people. Crow people have had buffalo on our land since 1939 and sometimes we run cattle too. No cows abort no problems. They are the connection to the earth that we need to survive in the spiritual world," said the Crow tribe chair.

"We are aware of the history," said the chairman wearily. "We are also aware that the Hartford family was given genetically pure buffalo for profit. We asked to come to the table and talk about this, but it happened behind closed doors. Native people will keep the lines pure, preserve our history.

There is going to be a big kill in a week on the first of February," he continued. "I say we do two things; we call the governor today to block the slaughter and we occupy Old Faithful Inn in protest, all 11 of us tribal leaders, until the Park agrees that the tribes take the buffalo back to the reservations. Our warriors were of a mind to burn it down, maybe we do that," he said, his smile reflected in his shiny eyes. "Damn, it is getting harder to demonstrate, they call you a terrorist.

"Draft our resolution, Looking Horse. Tell the governor that we want the buffalo protected so we will bring them home. Each tribe will take up to 400 pure blood buffalo from the park to the reservations. Our Wyoming brothers are not here today so don't know what they will do. Right now, this is about Montana. In exchange for that, we will preserve and protect the bloodlines and allow the buffalo to live in their natural state on the prairie. Tell them buffalo live in close family units. We cannot return the offspring to the Park. They will not stay, but will go looking for their family. Let Hartford repopulate the Park."

Looking Horse stared, his jaw dropping at the tribal chairman's words. Slowly a grin worked its way across his face. Standing up he slammed his fist on the table and let out a whoop.

"Now that's a plan I can approve of."

"Oh thank you, wise one," said the Chairman dryly. Looking Horse's face turned red.

"Bring plenty of blankets, food and a radio. We also need

 a way to communicate with the outside world. And firewood. I'm thinking a good bed might be important, my bones creak now with age," said the tribal chairman.

Looking Horse started making notes. "I think we should contact those people who have supported us in the past. That group out of DC who filmed the slaughter in '95 have kept in touch as well as the Buffalo Free folks. The National Buffalo Association and the Intertribal Bison Co-op would support us. The Fund for Animals wants to close Yellowstone to snow machines and prohibit cattle from grazing on public lands. They might come in."

Back in his office, Looking Horse let the phone ring. Old Man would want to hear the news. No answer. He'd call

after a while. Making a list on his yellow pad, he underlined media coverage – local, national and international. Europeans, especially the Germans, loved Indian people and their customs. Thank Buffalo Bill's Wild West Show for that. With that kind of spotlight attention, the Park Service would fold. They are not going to arrest the heads of eleven tribes. If he could find them, Gabe and Paul could join them. He had half a mind to leave them out in the cold for not listening to him, but, what the hell, he wasn't interested in being tied up in court defending them. This deal is going to work. Grinning, he thought to himself, this deal is going to make my career. But I've only got a few days to put the world spotlight on this before the buffalo slaughter starts.

##

"You ran out and left me. Those men could have hurt me," said Lucy as she pressed her face into the bars of the jail cell as she leveled her words at Red.

"So how come you're here? Just can't get enough of me, can ya." He came close and reaching out touched her cheek. "You could help me get out of here. They ain't even sure what they are holding me for. That FBI asshole had no business trussing me up like a damn turkey. House arrest for what! Just cause I know a couple of guys who are the real troublemakers."

Lucy stepped back, her cheek felt bruised. "I can't help you. I'm taking a chance just coming here."

"Yes you are and if you don't help me, I might remind them that you were with me for a good part of it."

"I didn't shoot anybody. You did and then you ran."

"That was an accident. My rifle discharged as I was chargin' through the door looking for your old boyfriend and that son-a-bitch Gabe. Do you know where they got to?"

"No," said Lucy. "And I am not going to help you, now or ever again."

"I'll give you a head start for old-times sake, but you better get before I call the jailer. But it ain't no matter, I'll be out of here in a couple of days. Let your boyfriend and his sidekick know ole Red's lookin for 'em."

"Why? Can't you let it be?"

Red turned and faded into the back of the cell. All she heard was a low laugh.

CHAPTER 20

# STAND OFF

"What a mess. Them damn Indians stripped all those beds and just threw 'em, mattress and all over the balcony. Left dirty dishes and clogged toilets. You'd think they would know the water was shut off," grumbled the park ranger. "Maintenance will have a hernia when they see this."

Hearing the big front doors creak, the rangers turned. Coming through the doors were what looked like a dozen Indians in full regalia including headdresses with feathers that reached to the floor.

Looking around the enormous room – at the fireplace that stretched four floors and the carved burl wood columns, and at the mess left by the occupation – the Blackfeet chairman said, "What is it our Buddhist brothers say – the road to enlightenment is to ‘chop wood, carry water.’ I think we do that now.”

With that he removed his head dress and without looking at the rangers picked up a mattress, shook it off and carried it up the long staircase. He was soon joined by the others. By mid-afternoon, Old Faithful Lodge was as before.

By evening, the lodge was stocked with food, gasoline for the generator and a stew was simmering on the stove. The ten men and one woman sat in council. Looking Horse had decided to stay in Billings to contact the media. His story was strong. The Feds had killed thousands. These buffalo could strengthen the herds already at the reservations, diluting strains from cattle. These revived herds would provide lean, healthy eating and help prevent the increase of diabetes. These pure ones would be saved for breeding and for reminding the people of their kinship with the buffalo.

Communication with the outside was difficult as cell towers weren’t allowed in the Park. WI-FI was available only at the grocery store, which was closed for the winter season. The Moccasin Telegraph didn’t stretch that far and smoke signals, joked the tribal leaders, would look too much like a fuming hotpot. The two-mile trip to the road where their vans were parked took some time, snowshoes or skis being the mode of transportation. But there was a cell signal there. Looking Horse expected to have the first media at the Lodge by the next morning even though fresh snow had fallen.

“I knew we should have left some of those mattresses

down here," said the Crow chair. Like the occupiers before them, the only way to stay warm and sleep was to stay close to the fireplace or in the kitchen. Air mattresses were quickly abandoned for the lodge's mattresses.

A blanket stretched between two pillars gave some privacy to the chair of the Northern Cheyenne. She was young to be in such a position and had spent the first year in office proving she was a warrior. If she were lucky, she would finish her second term before the tribe decided that change wasn't coming fast enough. The people were still hungry and many children lost in a haze of drugs. Hard to inspire a group of people whose only source of information circled inside. The old vision seekers, keepers of the sacred, the stories, the medicine, were mostly

gone. Their grandparents' memories were tainted, along with the knowledge of how to raise a healthy child connected to spirit by having spent their youth in white boarding schools. It is hard to know how to just be in this world. As an educated woman, she knew that saving the reservation often meant leaving it. The problem was getting a business in town to hire an Indian no matter how educated. So they came back to the rez, broke and disillusioned. And stayed. As a business major, she had some ideas that might spur economic development such as peer circle lending. But finding support for something that seemed simple, yet, she knew worked, took time.

The whole concept of commerce was foreign to reservations. Typically, there was only a grocery/gas station. No cafe, fast food, hardware stores, no place where a young person could get a job and understand what it took to run a business. Every time the government or private enterprise set up a business it hired white management who did not devise programs to train Indian people to move up in responsibility. At some point, the grant would end. The program would close. The white management would quit and the business – the experiment – would close. The people were left with an empty building and nothing learned. Rubbing her temples from an age old headache, she crawled in her sleeping bag. A minute later, she reached up and removed the blanket curtain, she was not going to block the heat. Let 'em look.

The next morning, as they gathered, the tribal chairs reminisced with stories of when their great grandfathers had moved with the buffalo herds. They talked of how it would be now, with the buffalo back home. Their ceremonies would give young people a sense of their connectedness.

"You know, this place might still be important to us," said the Cheyenne chairwoman. "Even on the rez there are cell towers on every high place where we go for our vision quests. The medicinal plants are mostly gone, but they might still be here. This environment might be a bridge to the natural order," said the Cheyenne chairwoman.

The men exchanged glances. "Sure, it is quiet now. It's 20 degrees below zero. Not too many tourists today."

As if summoned, the roar of snow machines could be heard getting close. A moment later the big doors pushed open. Looking Horse had definitely alerted the media.

##

"Well butter my butt and call me a biscuit, it's my Indian boys come callin'. How'd you get here," drawled Feral. "I suppose you think you are welcome, me pining for you, you who pelted me with mud and gravel in your getaway." Gabe staggered as Cisco jumped right into his arms, barking furiously.

"Feral, I didn't see ya," said Gabe. "We had to get while we could."

"Liar. You saw a chance to get rid of me and your dog. What do you want this time, I am out of automobiles, snow machines, all I got is a John Deere tractor. My neighbor won't lend me anymore vehicles on account of the company I keep."

"Now, Feral, Paul and me never took any of your vehicles. We just want to visit, catch the news, maybe a warm meal, a bed. You know, the stuff you should offer any friends."

Shaking her head, Feral opened the door wider. As Gabe slipped through, she stuck out her foot to trip him. He grabbed her and slapped her on the ass. Laughing she backed into the living room. Paul hurriedly closed the door against the cold.

"I'm surprised you aren't at Old Faithful with the chiefs. Or did they run you off," Feral said.

"Chiefs? Not many tribes have chiefs anymore. What are you talking about?" demanded Gabe. Rummaging through the refrigerator, he yanked off a chicken leg to gnaw on. Watching him, Paul figured manners be dammed, he was hungry and went for the other leg.

"Clearly your recent accommodations didn't have a TV, huh?" said Feral. "Incredible as it may be after your fiasco, the chiefs," 'chairmen' injected Paul, "are holed up in Old Faithful Lodge demanding that the Feds give them the park's buffalo to take back to the reservations. They want to take them home. I mean, I understand souvenirs, but this is ridiculous."

"Hot damn," said Gabe. "Are you kidding me?" Paul stood there with his mouth open choking on his chicken.

"Where were you, hiding under a rock? There has been a lot of media coverage." Feral reached in the refrigerator and pulled out the whole chicken, setting it on the table with a bang. Both men tore into it.

Looking up, Gabe grinned at Feral, "Don't get between a man and his bird."

"I'll give you the bird alright," snickered Feral raising her middle finger. Walking into the living room, she switched on the TV.

A close up of a newscaster, face red from the cold, stood in front of Old Faithful Lodge inviting the public to meet the chairs of Montana's eleven tribes. The reporter said the ten men and one woman had presented the governor with a petition demanding that purebred buffalo in Yellowstone Park be parceled out to the tribes. The governor's response was that it was a federal matter. "It's a federal park. Tribes may be sovereign nations, but they are under the Bureau of Indian Affairs and their land is held in trust with the federal government." He stated that the only time the state gets involved is when buffalo come out of the park and in contact with cattle. The state has a Brucellosis-free designation that saves ranchers from having to inoculate against the disease that causes cattle to abort.

"When are they gonna stop jawing about buffalo infecting cattle. It has never happened, ever," said Gabe. "I think the ranchers just don't want to share the public lands the cattle graze and pay a buck a year for."

The chair of the Tribal Council stepped into the camera, his black eyes slits in a heavily lined face. He was wearing full regalia complete with headdress and leather pants, heavy snow boots and a Hudson Bay blanket wrapped around his shoulders. He was flanked by the other chairmen similarly

attired. The chair from the Cheyenne reservation wore a full length coyote coat, the hood hiding everything but her black eyes.

"We are indigenous people. We are an endangered species. We are the rightful protectors of the buffalo – since creation – our brothers. We come to take the buffalo to our people, to the poor land you allotted us. White people have a way of dividing, creating lines and killing those who cross these lines. It happened when our people were pushed on reservations, it is happening now with the buffalo. Lines are not sacred. Killing, but for food, is not sacred. White people are killing the land, the water, the air, and in the process will kill themselves. Our land is all we have. In time, it will be like before, before the white man came and the world was balanced, all beings connected. For the buffalo, our people make our stand here today." With that, the group filed up the steps and through the huge doors, slamming them with a defiant thud.

By the following morning, the director of the National Park Service was on the phone to the President. "The governor of Montana is not going to do anything while the buffalo and the tribal chairs are in the Park."

"Hmm," replied the President, "I had planned to name him a department head, maybe in Interior. He just kissed that goodbye. This could become an international incident real quick if we make the wrong moves," said the President. "There are plenty of Americans, as well, who would raise hell. I say we listen to their demands, try to negotiate something but wait them out. They have tribal affairs to run, they won't stay there long. And isn't it damn cold there now?"

"With all due respect sir," said the NPS director, "Indians do not concern themselves with time or they wouldn't still be waiting for us to live up to the treaty agreements." The director's voice deepened. "There is another factor that could escalate the situation. A buffalo kill is scheduled in two days for those animals who have wandered outside the boundaries of the Park. The rangers have already notified the Fort Belknap Reservation whose turn it is to butcher and take the meat home to their people. This tribe has been waiting to receive a buffalo herd for their reservation for a long time. Their chair is part of the group at the lodge. My concern is the slaughter. When the rangers start shooting buffalo, it is really going to anger people."

"Well, don't shoot. And tell Montana that the animals have left the Park boundary, so now it's their problem."

"What about the chiefs holed up in the Lodge?"

"Dammit Roger, you get your ranger ass out of your office and on a plane and like I said, negotiate. Aren't there enough buffalo to give each Montana and Wyoming tribe a herd?"

"Probably sir, but it's more complicated. The ranchers in those areas will be up in arms, they don't want buffalo on range land. Many of them lease tribal land for grazing and worry about buffalo carrying disease. And the reservation land isn't fenced for buffalo."

"Well, in the words of Teddy Roosevelt, 'Speak softly and carry a big stick.'"

##

Gabe sat cross-legged in front of the TV going through the channels to see if there was any more news. His heart felt big in his chest. This must be what a blessing feels like he thought. "Taking the buffalo back to the rez makes more sense, a lot more sense, then trying to move people into the Park," he remarked. "We can build our herds. They live easy on the land."

"We can build a sustainable life for our people," said Paul. "This will wipe out hunger, diabetes and restore the spirit." Paul turned away dabbing at his eyes.

"We gotta build a fence first to keep 'em in," said Gabe with a laugh.

Feral curled up on the sofa, holding a slug of Jack Daniels. "Now I grant you, I haven't been a student of Indian, White relations, but do they really think the Feds will allow this? Even if they say they will, will they keep their word?"

"They will if the media will stay on it," said Paul.

"Paul, you spent too much time in the city," Feral said. "Out here a story lasts for a day or two, especially if it's about Indians and then it's over. But I am feeling the stirring of something in my gut, maybe my groin," she glanced over at Gabe and snickered. "When I had a life, before this self-imposed exile, I wrote some pieces for the Wall Street Journal. I know some people," she said taking a sip of her bourbon, her eyes glinting, a slow smile spreading over her face. "I know some people who would love to skewer the National Park Service for the lousy job they do maintaining the Parks and letting the concessionaires keep too much money. For this whole bullshit you told me about of keeping buffalo quarantined for the last three years while the tribes wait. I could have some fun with this and keep it square in the public eye. There are a lot of liberal hearts out there who would bleed for this. Tomorrow. Tonight I drink. It's too bad you guys don't."

The morning was clear blue and cold. Gabe sipped his coffee and fed the wood stove in the kitchen. Paul was outside probably doing some ritual, something that Gabe wished he could feel, understand more. His growing years were all about living through his mother's drunken rages while his dad prayed. But his father too was lit most of the time just to flatten the blows.

He felt Paul was lucky, he had his grandfather and his uncle, Old Man, to guide him. Old Man had tried to shield Gabe too, inviting him into the circle. Sometimes he came, searching his heart. Gabe had smoked the sacred pipe out of respect before they took the buffalo, but he found his true shield in the mountains. He thought about how certain places wrapped around him, in the good wild way. Just being there was a prayer. There he found his spirit.

Stomping the snow from his boots, Paul came in. “Shouldn’t we be heading out, get to the Lodge?”

“Yea,” replied Gabe. Wish we had heard something from Lucy about how that guy is doing.”

“Yea and what about her,” replied Paul. “She says she’s through with Red, but it hurts to have somebody just cut and run and leave you to the dogs.”

“Well, if ever there was a junkyard dog, it is ole Red. I just hope he stays in jail until this deal is done with the Park Service. Besides, if you want her, bet you can have her.”

“I have been up since well before the ass-crack of dawn, working for you,” said Feral looking up from her computer. “It’s two hours earlier in New York and I want to get a shot at tomorrow’s news. I’m giving this story to the Journal. If they don’t pick it up right now, I go to my contacts in broadcast. I got my people. I used to be hot stuff not that very long ago.”

“You still are tough lady,” Gabe said.

“You’re just talking sweet to me to get your way, but I like it," she said with relish.

"I hate to ask," said Paul tentatively.

"Oh shit, what do you need now," Feral said, "you took it all."

"How do you get to town for supplies."

"I been driving my dad's jeep, his special army jeep, that he put more love into restoring than he ever gave me. So no, you can't have that, he would truly kill me."

"We still got a truck. But it's been snowing up there, can't drive up to the lodge anymore on the hard pack. We need snowshoes, we need to walk a couple of miles in off the road and as you know, we were running for our lives and left our equipment at the Lodge," Paul said. Gabe leaned back against the kitchen counter and sipped his coffee, glad he hadn't asked.

"If I give them to you, you've got to take me," Feral said.

"No, don't you need to stay here with your computer and all?" Paul said. "Remember, there is no internet up there."

"True, but I will be along real soon."

"Got any gas money?"

"Get out!"

##

"Okay, here's the deal," said the Governor crossing his hands behind his head and leaning back in his chair. "The great state of Montana will provide the transport to the reservations. You, the Feds, put up the funding for buffalo-proof fencing. Because for every happy Indian, there will be a pissed off rancher and they are the ones who vote, so no free roaming buffalo."

"They are demanding that each reservation, all seven, get at least 400 additional head to assure genetic purity. That will strip the Park," said Roger.

"You were the ones who gave all those pure-bloods to Hartford, so go get them back," countered the Governor. "Besides, there are 11 tribes and since most of those sharing the seven reservations are historic enemies, each tribe will want their own herd."

"You are killin' me here," Roger said.

"Hey, its politics," said the Governor. "It's a cultural thing and who understands that."

"I have orders from the President to negotiate, wait them

out for a while."

"They are a patient people, but your trouble is going to come from outside," replied the Governor. "All the media attention. I don't want to look like the bad guy, so I don't have your back on this one. This will end up with the Indians winning. Soldiers lose."

"The President could have big plans for you," said Roger.

"I got my own plans. When my next term is over, I'm going to raise buffalo on my ranch," said the Governor hanging up the phone.

##

While the sight before him didn't match his dream, it was close enough for Paul. The tribal council had just adjourned following interviews by the media. Looking Horse had succeeded in attracting one photojournalist from the foreign press who published in France, Italy, Germany and Spain. No word yet from either the National Park Service or the Governor of Montana. Supporters of the cause were demonstrating in West Yellowstone, with a few hardy ones making their way to Old Faithful Inn. Gabe and Paul kept out of sight. It had been two days and no sign of Feral or Lucy.

A couple of the council members were talking about leaving. The Blackfeet Chairman asked them to stay two more days, making it a week since the occupation began. Every day the news carried a buffalo related incident. Mostly, it involved sympathizers, not Indian people or anyone who could make the necessary decisions.

##

Billy crunched a piece of chicken-fried steak, grease running down his chin. Jake shook his head, "You are such a mess, cousin."

"Hey, I haven't had good eats since before I ended up in the slammer," said Billy shoving another crispy chunk in his mouth. "Besides, I'm pissed that Red got away so don't mess with me."

"You hear that table over there talking German, I got an idea about how to mess with that Gabe and Paul."

"Why? They had no use for Red either, leastwise that's what you told me," Billy said.

"True, but they came down hard on my ass for no reason and I think we could poke a little fun here. Let's go over there, you be Gabe."

That night's broadcast carried a story about a group of Germans dressed as Indians who had sneaked onto Hartford's ranch and tried to stampede the buffalo with no real destination in mind. They told the sheriff that a couple of guys named Paul and Gabe, who were nowhere to be found, brought them here and told them that these buffalo belonged to the tribe and it was critical to move them out or they would be slaughtered. They had no idea buffalo could run so fast and up close, so big. That was enough to send them back to the motel in Bozeman. The search for Gabe and Paul intensified.

##

The fire just kept the mammoth room above freezing. Shivering, National Park Service Chief Ranger, Roger Harrison, pushed a sheath of papers across the table toward the Chairman. "I am authorized by the President himself to offer you the following terms, but the reservations also have to agree to the conditions."

The black eyes of the chairman never left the ranger's face as he slid the papers closer.

"Terms and conditions? What about agreements and our rights and your responsibilities."

"It's spelled out. You get buffalo and the funds to build the fences, but a percentage of the calves have to come back to the Park. This Park belongs to all people and their rights include seeing a buffalo when they tour the Park," Roger said.

"You know this, you have been told, buffalo live in family

units," the chairman said. "You tear apart a family and they will go wherever to reunite with their relatives. Would you want to never see your children, your cousins again? So it is with buffalo. You tried that in the Gallatin. They swam across the river every time back to their families. Go back to the President, tell him our terms and conditions. Remind him that in the winter of 1996-97 many Park buffalo starved to death and almost a thousand were shot when they foraged outside of the Park. And again in 2007-08, 1,600 pure-bred buffalo shot. Tell him his buffalo management plan looks a lot like –the old starve and – kill the Indian plan."

The afternoon sun barely touched the windows. With the frost build up on the inside, it muted the light to a cold blue. The Cheyenne chair had re-read their revised agreement four times now, her legal training reassuring to the council. No more treaties signed without legal advice, a hard lesson learned.

"The biology requires 400 animals. That means rounding up natural family groups to make up the total. Each tribe will do this. It will take time, but that's okay we need time to build the fences," injected Gabe.

"Right now there are 500 buffalo penned up with about 150 waiting to be shipped to slaughter. The only reason they are still here was trouble getting the trucks to move them. Of the 500, over 350 of the animals have been kept for over 3 years and are certified disease free. We could get those right away. A couple of the reservations, including the nearby Crow, have enough pasture to keep these first ones.

"What about the shooting planned for tomorrow? That has been stopped, right?"

"Even the dumbest government worker wouldn't let that happen now. Besides, there is an injunction."

##

Propped up with three pillows and snuggled under a feather comforter, Feral drank her hot toddy and watched the news. She had planned to go to the Lodge to see Gabe today, but the cold and waiting for a response from the Journal, kept her home.

Switching on the news, she watched in shocked astonishment at a special report stating that the US Interior Department had a state ruling set aside blocking the slaughter

of buffalo leaving the Park. The killing was to take place tomorrow. Clearly, somebody didn't get the memo. A spokesman for the Montana Livestock Association issued a statement applauding the action. Throwing back the covers, she raced to the telephone. This would get the Journal's attention.

##

The first shot sounded like a truck backfiring. Gabe rolled over, then suddenly, he sat up. There couldn't be a truck this close. That was a rifle. Trying to unzip his bag with one hand and grab his clothes with the other, the zipper stuck. In a fit of rage, he ripped open the bag and let out a yell. All around him heads peaked out.

"They're killing our buffalo. Those bastards are killing

our buffalo!" Strapping on his snowshoes, he plunged into the drifts that had built during the night. Paul was right behind him. In the lodge, the tribal chairs, seemingly dazed, were frantically putting on clothing. The Cheyenne woman grabbing her coat and boots went out the door, her long coat dragging in the snow, wrapped around her legs and tripped her. She got up, went back in, grabbed a jacket off a hook and took off again.

In the distance, Gabe could see a line of men in green uniforms kneeling in the snow, their rifles trained on a string of buffalo coming down the road avoiding the deep snow in the ditches. More shots. The buffalo had a glazed look. Their heads low, frost hung from their beards as they shuffled forward. They seemed not to notice when one of their own dropped beside them, it was as though they had surrendered. They just kept coming. And the men kept shooting. Seven, now ten lay bleeding in the snow. Between each shot and the thud, when the animal dropped, it was deadly quiet. A requiem.

Reaching the closest ranger, Gabe reached down and snatched up his rifle, so intent were the shooters, the others did not notice until Paul grabbed a gun and a guy let out a yell. Four rangers stood and pointed their rifles at Gabe and Paul.

Skidding and sliding up the road blowing its horn, a van slammed into a Park Service SUV parked on the shoulder before coming to a stop. All four doors opened at once. Even louder than their horn, the Governor of Montana yelled, "Back off, these buffalo are in my jurisdiction now and this is an executive order to stop."

Striding toward the men, the governor with his cadre of media, hollered to the shooters to stand down. Behind him stood the Park Superintendent looking everywhere but at the scene. Pointing to the dead animals the governor fumed, "Who told you to do this?

"Orders from the superintendent, sir," said the ranger.

"That would be me and I never gave that order." The ranger knew better than to contradict him.

More vehicles came around the curve. Within a matter of five minutes, there were a dozen media and over 20 protestors, all of them taking photos and video. A cameramen caught the look exchanged between the Governor and the Park Service.

"What are you going to do with these carcasses?" said the Governor.

"Waiting for the Indians who are going to butcher and take them," said the ranger.

Stepping forward, the chair of the Fort Belknap tribe of Assiniboine and Gros Ventre told them that his people would come, but that ceremony must be done to release the buffalo's spirit. They were not taken in the sacred way. If prayers of forgiveness, releasing the spirit of the buffalo were not asked, the meat would not sustain the people.

He invited them back to the Lodge where they could talk and he could get his prayer bundle and return to the kill site. With more animal rights people arriving, it seemed prudent to adjourn to the Lodge.

The kitchen was still the warmest room. The big table

worked as a conference table. The Cheyenne chair gave the tribal council chairman her revised copy of the proposal. The conditions set forth required funding for the fencing and the labor cost to erect it. Only tribal members could be hired. It also demanded supplemental animal feed for five years to allow the offspring to mature and breed. Only first cut alfalfa and no pesticides would be accepted. The issue of family units and genetic purity was addressed in the gathering and transporting the buffalo to the reservations. As she finished reading the draft, the ranger again stated his concern that the Park would be devoid of buffalo.

"I can see the headline now, 'Tribes strip Park of Buffalo," murmured the ranger. "Not good PR for anyone."

"Okay, what about the 500 you have penned up right now," injected Gabe. "We could start with those? You have tested 350 of them for years now. You know they are disease free so that can coddle the ranchers. We will also take the other 150 back to the rez. We are not afraid of Brucellosis."

"Before you can remove any buffalo to the reservations, that animal has to be tested and if diseased, shot. That is not negotiable," stated the ranger. "And, I don't have the authority to let you take them."

"We can pull this off," said the Governor.

He's become one with us Indians, thought Gabe ruefully. Maybe cause he is surrounded on all sides by Indians just like Custer.

"But we have to play by the rules," said the Governor.

"The science doesn't support it," said Gabe.

Staring at Gabe, the Governor squinted his eyes, looked away and back again. "Are you that crazy guy the cops are chasing? The one whose stupid idea it was to stampede Hartford's buffalo, poach an elk, kill a grizzly. Hey man, what are you doing here? Either hide or turn yourself in, or something. I can't talk to you and I don't have time to deal with you."

Gabe snickered and walked around behind the governor. Leaning against the wall he just could hardly keep from whooping out loud at the thought that his homeland would be the buffalo's homeland, his native brothers, whose hooves churned the soil restoring the grasses, the habitat for burrowing owls and prairie dogs and ferrets. Their spirit his.

Even though the big front doors were closed and bolted, the noise grew louder. The animal rights people had started a fire and set up tents. A boom box belted out drumming and singers who were clearly not of Plains tribes. In fact, the longer he listened to the high pitched voices, Paul doubted they were actual Indians from any place on this earth, but he was glad the supporters had come. The crowd had some German guys dressed as Indians. That was a new one for Paul. He had heard of their fascination of everything Indian, but seeing them made him feel embarrassed for them. They were wearing a costume, hoping to be clothed in the universal union. He wondered how they had gotten here and so soon. Wait until the sun goes down, along with the temperature. Right now, it felt almost balmy at 7 degrees above zero. 

The tribal leaders sat in silence, their demands made known. The Governor and the Park Superintendent talked quietly together. Gabe caught just a few words – words that made his head hurt, words like can't and regulation and the law. Words that meant delay or no go.

Coming back to the kitchen where the tribal leaders were eating breakfast, the Park Superintendent sat down and averting his eyes, told them he would lay out the situation. The bison were leaving the Park in big numbers. These animals could be and probably were diseased. Diseased bison could not be transported across Montana or allowed to wander on range land. Yellowstone holding pens were full. There weren't enough fences in Indian country at this time. The reservation's fences could not be built until spring when the ground thawed. Of the seven reservations, Crow had all the bison their range could handle and the Salish Kooteni had their own herd. Fort Belknap's Gros Ventre wanted bison and had some fencing as did Fort Peck's Sioux and Assiniboine tribes. The Blackfeet had the range but no bison and no fencing. Don't know about the Cheyenne or the Rocky Boy Reservation.

"I speak only for myself, but maybe my brothers. Yes, we have buffalo, but we, all tribes, even those who have buffalo, want Yellowstone stock for their genetic purity to build our herds," said Crow chair.

The Governor leaned forward placing his hands palm up on the table. "Got any ideas, cause I don't at least until spring."

The superintendent leaned back in his chair, arms crossed and gazed at the ceiling.

"I think you both go back to your official offices and we'll figure this out," said Gabe.

The Governor shook his head and said, "Not you again. You better figure out how to stay out of jail. Like I said, I can't talk to you or I will have to take some kind of action."

"That leaves killing maybe hundreds before end of winter and we are not going to let that happen," pressed Gabe ignoring the governor.

"We can visit about this in the spring," said the Governor. "Meanwhile the rangers will haze the bison back into the Park and only shoot if that fails."

"You know it fails," stormed Gabe. "A thousand dead buffalo one winter alone says it fails."

The two men picked up their briefcases. As the Governor walked toward the door he looked over at Gabe and quietly said, "You're already in trouble, so why not do what you can now," he said closing the door.

All heads turned to Gabe. "We're taking 'em, taking 'em home and here's how."

##

"As long as Red is in the slammer, I can't beat the shit outta him," said Billy. "I'm calling around and see who will make his bail."

The courtroom hearing was packed. Word that one of the Indians involved in the "Buffalo Caper," was getting out drew more media, buffalo supporters and relatives. Red felt like a celebrity. His attorney had cited the fact that the FBI had no right to detain him in his own home and all other acts that followed were the result of that. The judge listened with a look of disbelief, noting that shooting the trucker was not related. The lawyer said that was an accident. The bullet barely grazed the trucker and they would prove it in a court trial.

Earlier that week, the judge had granted bail to Leroy whose parole officer had put up the money. He had found him a job as a butcher and decided the work would do him more good than jail. Leroy managed to slip out the side door and was gone before the officer finished the paperwork.

The judge looked down on the crowd and wryly stated that he had had the dubious distinction of granting bail on not one but four people involved in this situation. He knew there was one more out there who hadn't been brought in yet and he could hardly wait to hear his version. He could only hope that he would preside over the joint trial – an efficiency that would save taxpayer money and hopefully collaborate at least someone's version of the story.

Billy and Jake watched from across the street as Red left the courthouse.

"Let him think everything is just happy as fry bread, then we will teach that son-a-bitch just how Sioux takes enemy."

Sitting in that courtroom, Red had an idea. The judge was referring to Gabe when he mentioned one more out there. Why not finger Gabe and help the cops find him. It would be almost as good as me personally kicking his ass and it might give me some leverage with my own charges. Maybe both. Kick ass first, then call cops. It sure would put a smile on ole Red's face, he thought. Get in a few licks with Paul too, he is sure to be hustlin' my woman.

## CHAPTER 21

# LOAD EM UP, HEAD EM OUT

"Every time a family of buffalo leaves the park, we are going to load them and truck them to a reservation," said Gabe, his gaze taking in each tribal chair. "Every tribe has stock trucks. We park them in Gardiner with a driver and I stay here and watch. Sometimes I can push a herd out but we need to be ready and quick. My sense is we got to do this through May before the snow lets up enough for them to find forage in the park. We start building our fences now and come spring, get the rest.

"So, who can get trucks here now? We take this first bunch, the ones they have penned up for three years. That will take at least four, probably five semis. Then we hide 'em."

"We have stock trucks close. I could send for them this morning and load tonight," said the Cheyenne woman. "But my people will want some meat. We have a lot of hungry families this winter. We can take a few marked for slaughter."

"How about the rest of that herd they are going to ship to slaughter, let's take them too," said Paul.

For a minute or two no one spoke. Then the Crow chair cleared his throat, "Our buffalo are certified free of disease, so I can't bring these there."

"We will take them. I can put them on my uncle's place, the Gro Ventre chairman said. "We will move them back up the valley."

"Bad idea," said Gabe. "I'm not afraid of disease, but it will get everybody riled up and could screw up our spring gathering."

"What's the matter Gabe, you never play by the rules," said Paul.

"This matters," said Gabe. "We don't want to start out pissing off ranchers any worse than we are going to. No point in it. We'll take the 350 that are already certified and be ready when others come out of the park before the rangers spot them and quarantine them or shot 'em."

"Okay, then, let's let them loose and push them back into the park, said Paul. "At least they have a chance."

"It is agreed then," said the Tribal Chair.

Feral backed the jeep out of the garage, just catching a glimpse of movement as she cleared the door. Must have been snow falling off the roof, she thought. Easing the clutch, she turned around and headed down the plowed road. Maybe with all the traffic packing the snow, she could still drive right up to the lodge. She needed her own getaway rig close this time in case Gabe ran out again.

After watching her pack up food and gear in the jeep, Red figured he had plenty of time to enjoy himself, knowing that she must be headed for the Lodge and Gabe. Pulling the comforter around his shoulders he thought for a minute about taking off his boots, but what the hell, by the time he finished trashing this house, a little mud on the sheets wouldn't much matter. Plus, the sandwich and bourbon made him real sleepy. Gabe could wait. That bitch Feral is goin' to get some now.

##

When the first trucks pulled into the holding area, Gabe looked at Paul and shook his head. These were not semis pulling stock long-haulers, these were pickups pulling horse trailers and a few cattle trailers. At this rate, it would take a lot more rigs. Not a problem, the Cheyenne chair assured them. Plenty would show up. They would take maybe twenty head for their trouble and truck the certified disease-free to Belknap and Crow. The tribes who wanted them could go there. The only luck they had was the holding pen had a chute and a ramp to funnel the animals onto the truck.

Finding guys who even knew how to load cows was going

to be tough, Gabe told Paul. While there were still some of the protestors hanging around, they were mostly college kids and not farm kids. He hoped the drivers who brought the rigs knew what they were doing. "We crowd 'em and they will start tearing each other up with their horns and you too if you get in the way. They are not used to being loaded, they aren't like cows." Gabe also wanted to keep their activities low key since this was supposed to be an under-the-cover-of-darkness operation.

Mama was not going to budge. Her calf was standing sideways of the chute in front of her and she wasn't going anywhere. "Is that calf stuck, why won't the little bastard turn?"

"Why Paul, I never heard you cuss before and at your spirit animal," snickered Gabe. It was almost midnight, fifteen below zero and they were only about half way through. The crew which was made up of five guys including them and three of the tribal chairs, plus a driver, were all were covered in buffalo shit and mud. They were bone weary, but it had to be done before the sun came up and it would take all of that time. The animals were agitated and kept circling, pushing the young ones to the protection of the center.

They had to prod the buffalo toward the chute by hanging on the fence and leaning over and poking them with a pole. Mostly the animals ignored them, the stick felt like a fly on their thick hide. But if they could get one or two moving in the right direction, others would follow. Even if they had a horse, it was too crowded to use one. Finally, one of the drivers brought a prod and it helped a little.

They had a fire going with hot tea brewing and Feral had brought cookies and sandwiches. The woman always brought food thought Gabe. It kept her from being thrown out of most places. She was back at the Lodge probably voicing her opinion of the whole gig to anyone still awake.

Paul, warming his hands over the flame glanced up. Just as he did, he saw a guy wearing a hood come up behind Gabe who was on the fence. The hooded figure grabbed Gabe's feet and pushed him over the side of the pen into the milling herd. Paul stood dumfounded for a second and then ran to the fence yelling for help, his voice barely carrying over the noise of the animals. Climbing up the fence he saw Gabe flat on his back, the huge animals crowding around him, their eyes wild, showing white. Gabe wasn't moving. He didn't look dead, but he didn't move. Paul waved his arms to the others on the fence to stop pushing the herd. One-by-one they did except for one guy who kept up prodding and yelling. Paul looked again, how come there were still four guys besides him on the fence.

Was the one who had dumped Gabe still here on the fence making sure Gabe got trampled? Paul didn't know what to do. Go after whoever was trying to get Gabe or help Gabe, and how was he going to do that?

Paul leaned over the fence again calling to Gabe when he felt himself being projected over the top and landing on Gabe. Leering down over the top of the fence was Red. "A lucky two-fer-one. This will teach you to mess with ole Red."

"I'm gonna mess with ole Red damn betcha," said Billy the Sioux stepping out from behind a truck. "I'm gonna pistol whip the shit out of ole Red and you ain't getting away this time. You left me for the cops and cause of you, I ended up in jail." Grabbing Red's legs, he dragged him off the fence with Red hitting each steel row with his head. "You kept my meat," said Billy. "Cause of you, I lost that bear picture and a real good buffalo robe. You won't sneer at the Sioux never again." Reaching down to pull Red up, a shot fired and Billy hit the ground. Red jumped up, jammed his pistol in his pants and took off running. Lucy opened the pickup door knocking Red flat. Now Jake was on him, flogging him with a tire iron.

Red yelled, "Okay, ya got me." Seeing Lucy through the blood streaming down his face, he said, "You still want ole Red, don't cha!"

The buffalo spooked and tightened their circles.

Two of the tribal chairs were tying rope together to hoist the men out while the third hung over the fence talking to Paul. Gabe seemed to be coming around. He started to get up and then realized where he was. Looking over at Paul, he said, "This ain't right. What are we doing down here?"

Paul moved slowly on all fours until he was up against the wall of the pen. "Can you move?" he said. Just then Feral swung her leg over the fence and stared down. "What in the hell are you two doing down there. Paul, you coward, get over there and help Gabe." Feral's shrill voice seemed to agitate the herd even more. 

Looking up, Gabe and Paul yelled in unison, "Shut your mouth, woman!"

Nobody noticed the big bull buffalo who was pawing the ground, lowering his head and snorting in the direction of Paul and Gabe. Suddenly Old Man appeared in front of the bull, singing the buffalo song, calling the buffalo spirits.

Gabe tried to crawl over to Paul, but his leg was broken from hitting the chute cross bar on the way down.

Feral started over the fence, muttering, "Saving Indians is a full-time job."

The tribal chair held her back. "Stay up here. We bring them up here, then you help."

Lowering the rope to Paul, he told him to hang on. Paul looked over at Gabe, took the rope and started to walk his way up the fence. Suddenly he jumped back down, yelled, "Give me some slack, we got to get Gabe out of here first. I'll make a sling."

Old Man appeared to be humming to the big bull who continued to blow snot and shake his immense head.

Feral, climbing over the fence to drop a rope, found herself following it head first as a loop caught on her boot heel pulling her over. She landed on Gabe. Looking at her, a grimace of pain crossing his face, Gabe said, "You never been anything but trouble. A sassy-mouth. Now get off me. Go find me a vehicle or bake brownies or something."

Paul tied the sling between Gabe's legs and around his

waist and told the others to pull him up. Slowly Gabe was lifted from the pen, his injured leg hitting the fence with each thrust.

Looking up Paul saw horror on the faces above him. "Oh no," a voice screamed. The two men pulling Gabe stopped in midair.

Turning, Paul saw Old Man being tossed in the air by the bull landing at the beast's feet. The crazed animal slammed his immense head down hard to crush him. Old Man rolled. Paul drug him to the wall. Looking up, Old Man said, "That one mad buffalo. He not like my singing."

##

Back in the Lodge's warm kitchen, Billy the Sioux and Red lay on cots with Gabe between them. The Cheyenne council woman, who was raised patching up three wild brothers, was tending to their wounds. The council chairman had set his own broken leg once so he figured he could take care of Gabe's. And he did. Gabe blacked out with the pain, but came around with a jolt of whiskey. Choking and gasping for air, he croaked, "The fix is worse than the break."

The chairman laughed and thumped Gabe on the back, "Be a warrior, not a whiner."

Feral, standing over Red, shone a light in his eyes.

"With any luck, you will have a concussion, forget you're an asshole, or die of blood poisoning. All in favor of the latter, blink." Red's face was already turning black and blue, adding to the green from his previous run-in with Gabe. He was sure his collar bone was broken after Jake hit him with that tire iron. Nobody seemed in a hurry to take him to the doctor. Gabe said they had to finish loading first. "Screw those damn buffalo, been nothin' but trouble from the git-go. Nobody gives a shit about ole Red." Feral laughed and kicked the leg on the cot. "Billy and Jake here will take care of you."

Billy had a small hole in his calf, but the bullet had missed the bone and passed through. "So I get another shot at ole miserable Red," said Billy, "this time real close up." Crawling out of bed, he hobbled over to Red's cot and propping a stool by the bed poked Red in the chest with a skinning knife.

Red closed his eyes tight and moaned, "Gabe, we go way back. We Blackfeet. We brothers. Tell this Sioux to go home. We even."

"We even! You gotta be shittin' me," said Billy. "Every time you open your eyes I am gonna be sittin' here till I get tired of ya, then I'm gonna cut something off, old Indian trick."

Jake came in from outside and seeing his brother leaning over Red's cot, said, "Leave a piece for me."

Outside the loading continued. Only a couple of stock trucks were left with three more on the way from the Crow Reservation. The darkness faded to a pale grey. The sun, as if weary of winter, thrust its fragile beams across the land slowly gaining strength.

Paul stood on the fence counting buffalo with Lucy beside him. Touching his arm, she said, "Are you done with looking? Are you ready to just be here?"

"If I can be with you," he said, wrapping his arm around her.

"Hey you two, fooling around on the job," snickered Gabe. He had somehow snuck out of the lodge and into the pickup without Feral catching him.

"How did you do that, you can't be on that leg," said Paul jumping off the fence and jerking open the truck door.

"Well, there was a rake handle and I hopped on one foot after a shot of whiskey for go power. Just enough for medicinal use. We got to finish and there isn't much time to get them off the highway to Belknap and Crow before the park rangers figure it out."

Old Man climbed in the cab. "Gabe, a one-legged Indian not gonna be a good buffalo boss. We are going to doctor. You

take Paul's wallet, his picture. White people think all Indians look alike."

"We leave Red and Billy here together, there will be more blood," Gabe said. "Feral might really do something if Billy or Jake don't finish him first. Course that could take care of the ass-kickin I'm gonna give him just as soon as I got both legs under me."

"Red pretending coma, Billy wants eyes open so he sees scared Red. We be back before play acting over," said Old Man. "Nobody gonna kill nobody, just scare real bad."

Glancing in his rearview mirror, Gabe saw Feral approaching, calling his name and cussing his ancestors and unborn children. "Let's get before that she-cat climbs in this truck."

“Yah,” said Paul, “kinda reminds me of the wolverine. It will take a hatchet to get her off you.”

“Shit,” said Gabe hitting the brakes, “we are going to need her ranch until spring once the tribal chairmen leave Old Faithful. The snowmobilers aren’t pressing charges, but the Feds are pissed over the bear, elk and occupying the Lodge. They’re gonna get their back up over us taking these buffalo. Besides, she cooks and seems to like my dog. Leaning out the window, he yelled, “Feral, woman, get in.”

Paul opened the door for her and pulling Feral’s face to meet his, he said, “You get back here and help move these buffalo, we can’t do this without your sass.”

“Don’t I know it!”

THE END

Or is it?

# AUTHOR'S BIO

Shari comes from a long line of renegades beginning with her family fleeing from France to Quebec in the 16th century. They immediately moved West and are credited with having the first white child born in Saskatchewan and in Alberta. Her grandfather was a leader under Louis Riel in the 1885 Metis Resistance taking on the English and the Scots in Canada over native land rights. Shari's father was a hunter and photographer in Alaska.

Venturing is in Shari's DNA. From Montana, she went to Kodiak Island, AK, right after the quake. She lived in a skid-shack with a 10-month old baby and no running water. Shari feels that the high points of her career include serving as PR director for the CM Russell Museum and the Buffalo Bill Historical Center and as MT's first cultural specialist working with the tribes.

She now lives in Fromberg, MT (population 444) with husband David, four chickens, two Lop rabbits, kittens, two Shih Tzu and a couple of Pygmy goats. She is working on two more novels.

Made in the USA
Charleston, SC
05 December 2016